Praise for Eric Nylund and the
Mortal Coils Series

"Nylund has hit his stride, piling on the █████ █oments, but never losing sight of th█ ████████ ████ations that made the first b█ ████ ██████

—████████ *█ekly*

"A sparkling and ████████ █████ ████ ███████ous, intriguing events ██████ ████ ████████ ██s *Weekly*

"A genuinely engag██ ████████ █ that should appeal to a wide variety of rea██ ███om urban fantasy lovers to fans of myth-based fiction."   —*Library Journal*

"The exciting first novel of what promises to be an epic series."   —Greg Bear,
multiple Hugo and Nebula Award–winning
author of *Eon* and *Moving Mars*

"*Mortal Coils* is a young-adult urban fantasy . . . a wonderful entry into this genre . . . a truly fast-paced thrill ride that is both rich in story telling and intellectually fun to play with."   —*Fantasy Literature*

"A brilliant blend of urban fantasy, fantastic atmosphere, and ancient mythology."   —*BSC*

"A hair-raising tale . . . finely crafted characterizations."
—*Booklist*

"An exciting adventure filled with twists and turns."
—Marcia Berneger, *MyShelf.com*

"The writing . . . is just superb. [Nylund] really knows what he's doing as a writer, which is obvious from the very first page, and is a major reason why *Mortal Coils* is such an impressive book. . . . *Mortal Coils* will be remembered as the author's magnum opus. Just a magnificent blend of magic, myth, dysfunctional families, imagination, and storytelling, *Mortal Coils* is a future classic."
—*Fantasy Book Critic*

OTHER BOOKS BY ERIC NYLUND

Pawn's Dream
A Game of Universe
Dry Water
Signal to Noise
A Signal Shattered

HALO® NOVELS

Halo®: The Fall of Reach
Halo®: First Strike
Halo®: Ghosts of Onyx

MORTAL COILS SERIES

Mortal Coils

ALL THAT LIVES MUST DIE

ERIC NYLUND

TOR®

A TOM DOHERTY ASSOCIATES BOOK
NEW YORK

ALL THAT LIVES MUST DIE

A Tor Book
Published by Tom Doherty Associates, LLC
175 Fifth Avenue
New York, NY 10010

www.tor-forge.com

Tor® is a registered trademark of Tom Doherty Associates, LLC

ISBN 978-0-7653-6291-9

First Edition: July 2010
First Mass Market Edition: December 2011

Printed in the United States of America

0 9 8 7 6 5 4 3 2 1

*For Syne, the passion of my life and the one
woman I'd go to Hell and battle the
Legions of the Damned for*

&

*For Kai, your father promises he will never
make you go to the Paxington Institute
(unless you want to)*

ACKNOWLEDGMENTS

My gratitude to the following people for their help, confidence, and being some of the best friends a writer could have: Richard Curtis, Tom Doherty, Alexis Ortega, Eric Raab, and John Sutherland.

EDITOR'S NOTE

We at Tor have received numerous requests to publish the many-volume set of *Gods of the First and Twenty-first Century,* as well as the notorious *Golden's Guide to Extraordinary Books* and, of course, the apocalyptically difficult to obtain and decipher *Mythica Improbiba.* At this time, however, the rights for these rare books (and others within *All That Lives Must Die*) reside with academic institutes, religious organizations, and private collectors. While excerpts have been graciously provided for Mr. Nylund's footnotes, the remaining bodies of these works are fated to remain in obscurity (and please, please stop sending me e-mail and letters about this).

Eric Raab
Editor, Tor Books
New York

QUEEN GERTRUDE
Do not for ever with thy vailed lids
Seek for thy noble father in the dust:
Thou know'st 'tis common; all that lives must die,
Passing through nature to eternity.

HAMLET
Ay, madam, it is common.

QUEEN GERTRUDE
If it be,
Why seems it so particular with thee?

WILLIAM SHAKESPEARE
Hamlet (ACT 1, SCENE 2)

ALL THAT
LIVES
MUST DIE

PROLOGUE

❦

WHAT I DID OVER MY SUMMER VACATION *by Fiona Paige Post*

This summer, my brother and I joined the League of Immortals. One minute, I'm a homeschooled hermit; the next, I'm a fledgling goddess-in-training and the newest member of the Order of the Celestial Rose.

You'd think, being an actual goddess, I'd end up with killer Botticelli hair. No luck there, I'm afraid.

Let me start at the beginning.

Gods and fallen angels exist.

And they don't get along.

Despite this, sixteen years ago—Atropos, the Eldest Fate, and Lucifer, Prince of Darkness, fell in love.

They're my mother and father.

When my twin brother and I were born, my mother didn't want either side of the family finding us. Neither the gods nor fallen angels treat their nieces and nephews well: turning them into animals, trees, weeping stones, or casting them into pits of eternal torture. Nice, huh?

So for fifteen years, my brother, Eliot, and I were hidden from our relatives and raised to think we were nerdy and normal.

The Immortals found us, however, and to decide which family we belong to—diabolical or divine—they subjected us to three life-or-death tests (what they prosaically called heroic trials).

Long story short: We passed their tests and came out divine.

It wasn't all happy endings, though. My father's side of the family still wanted us. The Infernal Lord of All That Flies, Beelzebub, almost killed us and dragged our souls to Hell. That ended in a huge fight in Del Sombra (where we used to live); I killed Beelzebub, and the entire town burned to the ground.

Our father said he still wants to get to know us, but I don't think Mother is going to let him.

I agree. I don't trust him.

After all this, my brother, mother, great-grandmother, and I went to San Francisco, and we've barely moved into a new place in time for school.

It has been a tumultuous summer. I just want to settle down and begin at the Paxington Institute so I can figure out how I fit into this new world where legends are real.

September 22, San Francisco

WHAT I DID OVER MY SUMMER VACATION by Eliot Zachariah Post

This summer, I found out that my father and mother are alive. My sister and I spent our entire lives thinking they were dead, told that they were drowned in a boat accident.

One more thing: Our mother is the goddess Atropos, and our father is Lucifer, Prince of Darkness.

Mother's side of the family are gods and goddesses in the League of Immortals. They smile at you, but you can see them thinking behind those smiles, wondering how you fit in their orderly view of the world.

And Dad's side of the family? Not so wonderful, either. They tried to kill me and my sister, Fiona. They also managed to poison Fiona with a box of magical chocolates.

Besides our parents, we discovered another important thing this summer: We inherited special powers from our families.

Fiona can cut with a thread stretched between her fingers, kind of like a wire cheese slicer. When I say "cut," I mean she can cut through anything when she puts her mind to it: cinder block walls, a solid steel vault door, even a person. I'm not sure how she keeps the thread from cutting off her fingers. She doesn't talk much about it.

I think it scares her. I know it scares me.

I learned how to use the violin. My father showed me the basics, but I play like I've been practicing all my life . . . and my music makes things happen. Magical things, like conjuring a fog filled with ghosts or charming a million hungry sewer rats so they wouldn't eat me.

Then, once, I got a glimpse of the end of the world. I played a song about the end of things, which I call "The Symphony of Existence." If that sounds dangerous, it was, but I had to, believe me, because I was facing the Infernal Beelzebub, Lord of All That Flies, who was trying to part my right side from the left with a gigantic obsidian knife.

When I played that song, I felt the world come apart around me, and I heard the death rattle of the universe as protons and neutrons and electrons tore into smaller subatomic bits . . . and then into void.

I still hear it in my dreams. It worries me some-times.

I've learned a lot this summer, but I'm ready to learn more at Paxington and find out what I'm supposed to be doing with these amazing and dangerous gifts.

September 22, San Francisco

———

Eliot watched and worried as his sister read his essay.

Her brows furrowed.

Eliot knew people liked his writing style better, but Fiona was good at putting facts together and impressing people with her logic. Besides, her essay pretty much told the entire story of what had happened to them this summer. He hoped the teachers at Paxington read his paper first.

"Well?" he asked her. "What do you think?"

"Just a second." She held up a hand, rereading from the top of the page.

Eliot paced. Sunlight filtered into his new bedroom from the garden. Outside were rows of pink and yellow daisies, and beyond, he could make out misty San Francisco Bay—a spectacular view.

Inside their new house, however, especially in his bedroom, the view was not so spectacular—crowded with mountains and mazes of cardboard U-Haul boxes, each one filled with a hundred pounds of books. If there was the slightest shudder from the San Andreas Fault, Eliot knew he'd be buried under an avalanche of Chaucer, Twain, and Shakespeare.

Fiona looked up from his essay and brushed her long, dark hair from her face. "You don't have *all* the facts," she said. "You should have added something about your *girlfriend*."

"She wasn't my girlfriend," Eliot replied.

Fiona meant Julie Marks, the girl he had met this summer, the girl he had liked an awful lot. She'd even kissed him . . . but then ended up leaving. Every time he thought about her, he felt that he had done something to drive her away. Fiona had never liked Julie, for some reason.

He glared at his sister, suddenly irritated.

Then he understood: Fiona wasn't trying to be mean on purpose. She couldn't help it. Anyone would be a little nasty if they looked the way she did this morning.

Normally, he and his sister had to wear their great-grandmother's handmade clothing—bad enough because it looked like something out of the "wrong clothes that didn't fit" catalog.

Today was worse. They had on their new Paxington school uniforms.

The new clothes looked fine when Eliot and Fiona had first gotten them: khaki slacks for him, pleated tartan skirt for his sister, white button-down linen shirts and navy blue blazers for them both. No ties, thank goodness—they probably would have strangled themselves. Fiona had stockings and flats. He had leather loafers with no heels that made him look (if possible) shorter than usual.

All well and good, Eliot supposed . . . if you actually knew how to wear such things.

But Fiona had never owned, let alone worn, a pair of stockings. Her skinny legs looked like crumpled caterpillars that had cocooned themselves and died there. Add to this that no one in the Post family knew how to use an iron (or at least, no one was willing to let the doddering 104-year-old Cecilia near an iron), and they both ended up looking like they had slept in their new uniforms.

Eliot shifted underneath his blazer—one size too big for him—and felt just as uncomfortable and annoyed as his sister must. He exhaled a great sigh, smelling something off. Maybe his clothes should have been washed first.

This was just what they needed today. He ran a hand through his hair, whose cowlicks, as usual, resisted any attempts at grooming. Not only would they have to deal with dozens of strange new students on their first day at school, but they also looked like dorks.

Eliot tapped Fiona's essay and told her, "I see you didn't mention Robert, either."

"What's to mention?" Fiona said. "We haven't seen him in two months."

Robert Farmington was the boy Fiona had met this summer. They weren't exactly boyfriend and girlfriend, but there had been *something* between them. He had been a Driver for their uncle Henry in the League of Immortals . . . before Robert got fired.

Fiona had a far-off look in her eyes—which sharpened to a glare that she aimed directly at Eliot. "Cupulate temporal cranium?" she asked.

This was the game they played to get back at each other: vocabulary insult.

Eliot ran over the line in his head, trying to figure out what she had meant. Brain . . . cranium . . . something about his head.

Temporal? Did that mean "time"? No, the bone on the side of the head was the "temporal" part of the skull.

But *cupulate?* He didn't have a clue . . . unless she

was making it simple in order to throw him. *Cupulate* could just mean "cup shaped."

She meant his ears.

They stuck out, and she knew how sensitive Eliot was about them.

"At least I need a cup, handles or not," Eliot replied, "to hold *my* brain."

That was a weak comeback, so he added: "Countenance of verruciform," and then with a sweeping gesture down to her toes, "vermiform locomotion borne."[1, 2]

Fiona puzzled over that a moment, and then her face reddened.

Good. It was pretty easy to figure out. Eliot had wanted her to get it.

"No fair," she said. "That's two vocabulary words at once."

She said this, despite having just used two herself.

"Breakfast!" Cee called from the kitchen.

Eliot sniffed the air and realized that the "off" smell he'd detected before was stronger, and now recognizable—half-cooked oatmeal and carbonized bacon.

Fiona spotted Eliot's rusty alarm clock in the corner. Her eyes widened. "We're going to be late!" She rushed out, bumping a tower of boxes, almost knocking them over.

Of course they were going to be late for their first day of school. That would be the perfect start to this morning. Eliot scrambled after her. There was no way she was getting to the kitchen first to pick out the few edible bits from Cee's cooking.

---

1. Verruciform: having the shape of a wart. —Editor.

2. Vermiform: worm shaped. —Editor.

THE FIRST DAY
OF SCHOOL

1

❧

NEW RULES

Fiona scrambled over the cool terra-cotta tiles and skidded to a halt in their new dining room. Bookshelves and half-built china cabinets were constructed along the walls. Unlike their old apartment in Del Sombra, this room had enough space for shelves *without* crowding the glorious picture window and its built-in seats.

The window framed the Golden Gate Bridge in the distance. Early-morning light spilled through and made the plaster cornices of the room glow gold.

Cee carried in two trays from the kitchen. Their 104-year-old great-grandmother wore a brown dress with lace ruffles and looked like she belonged in a nineteenth-century silver daguerreotype with her hair pulled up tight and pinned in place. Some things would never change. That was okay. Cee, shaking and smiling, was always there for them.

"Let me help," Fiona offered.

"No, no, my darlings," Cecilia replied. "Just sit and eat. You have a momentous day ahead of you."

With trembling arms, she set a platter of smoking

black bacon on the table, and another platter with bowls of lumpy half-cooked oatmeal.

"Don't you two look splendid in your uniforms?" Cee kissed Eliot on the cheek and then Fiona. It felt like the brush of dry leaves. She then went back into the kitchen.

"Thanks, Cee," Fiona said, and tugged on her stockings. How could something so tight fit so poorly?

"Thanks," Eliot murmured. He sat and dragged a bowl closer, grimacing.

Fiona shot him a look. Cee *did* try. It wasn't her fault she no longer had a sense of smell or taste.

Eliot stirred the mixture in front of him in an attempt to make it palatable.

She pulled a bowl closer as well and segregated the inedible bits from the stuff that looked like it could be choked down.

Sometimes having a severed and only partially repaired appetite had its advantages.

Fiona spooned the lumps into her mouth. It tasted like sawdust . . . but then almost everything did these days. She knew she had to force herself to eat, or she'd faint from malnutrition.

So she chewed until she could swallow the oatmeal without gagging.

In fact, if she didn't force herself to feel something, she didn't feel much of anything. That was because when she'd cut her appetite to save herself from those addictive Infernal chocolates . . . she cut deeper . . . cut part of the connection to her emotions. Like what she felt for Robert. It was so unclear. Did she really miss him? Or had it been some crush brought on by their shared adventures this summer?

No, there *was* something there.

It was complicated, because she was now part of the

League of Immortals, and Robert had just been fired by the League. *Fired* meaning that some Immortals had a grudge against him, and if they ever saw him, it might be the end of his life.

How could she be with someone who was endangered by her very presence?

She watched Eliot struggle with his oatmeal, his face contorting through various shades of discomfort and strangulation as he swallowed. She *did* feel some tiny punitive pleasure from that.

Vermiform locomotion borne, huh? She tried to smooth her stockings again, but it was hopeless. Her legs *did* look like two wrinkled worms.

Outside, fog covered the sun. The golden light tinged iron gray, and the temperature in the room dropped.

Audrey descended the spiral staircase that led to her office. She joined them at the table.

She wore faded jeans, chamois soft boots, and a deep blue silk blouse that matched the color of San Francisco Bay. Diamond studs adorned her earlobes and flashed cold rainbows upon her throat and slicked-back silver hair. She carried a slender briefcase. She was the picture of grace and understated elegance, and looked perfectly at ease in their new surroundings.

But it wasn't only the new clothes that made Audrey look different today.

When Fiona came back from her summer vacation, this woman was no longer the "grandmother" she had known for the last fifteen years. That masquerade was over. She was her mother now and the goddess Atropos, and *both* titles seemed equally perplexing to Fiona.

"Good morning, Audrey," Fiona said. She couldn't call her Grandmother anymore, and the word *Mother* caught in her throat, so Fiona had settled on Audrey.

"Good morning," Eliot echoed.

"Good morning, children," Audrey replied. She poked carbonized bacon with a fork and then decided to pour herself a glass of juice. "I've ordered the books you'll need for Paxington . . . assuming you do well enough on the entrance examinations today. I have every confidence that you will."

If she had every confidence, then why even mention it?

Those books—which would join the thousands and thousands already here—had to be ordered because many of their books had pages crossed out to the point of unreadability. Those were the books on mythologies, legends and folklores, ghost stories, tales of demons and gods—all omitted because their mother had the notion that she could hide Fiona and Eliot from the truth . . . and hide the truth from them.

"I guess . . . ," Eliot started, but his voice died. He swallowed and tried again. "I guess that means Rule Fifty-five doesn't apply anymore?"

Rule 55 was one of the 106 household rules that governed every aspect of Fiona's and her brother's lives. It was the "nothing made up" rule.

RULE 55: No books, comics, films, or other media of the science fiction, fantasy, or horror genres—especially, but not limited to, the occult or pseudosciences (alchemy, spirituality, numerology, etc.) or any ancient or urban mythology.

Audrey looked at Eliot as if he spoke a language she didn't understand.

How typical. Audrey was very good at telling them what to do—not so good at listening to anything they had to say.

"That's why you're sending us to Paxington, right?" Fiona asked. She worked very hard to keep anger from creeping into her voice. She made herself sound polite, quizzical—keeping this discussion on an intellectual level. "I mean, you're sending us there to learn about our family, their history, and how we're supposed to fit into this world."

Audrey blinked. "Yes, Rule Fifty-five is naturally abolished. You must learn everything that has been omitted from your education as quickly as possible."

Fiona nodded and kept her face an impassive mask, hiding her glee.

Audrey had never *lifted* a rule. The only changes to the rules for as long as Fiona had lived were *additions*.

She and Eliot would have to be careful. They couldn't push. Audrey tended to push back ten times harder when confronted with the slightest force.

As if sensing the precise *wrong* thing to say, Eliot leaned forward and asked, "So, what about all the other rules?"

Fiona could have killed him.

"We will revisit them on a case-by-case basis." Audrey took a sip of orange juice. "*If* necessary."

"So then, what about Rule Thirty-four?" Eliot said. Both his hands gripped the edge of the dining table.

Fiona gave him a kick—hard.

Eliot flinched, but he didn't look away from Audrey. Rule 34 was the "no music" rule.

RULE 34: No music, including the playing of any instruments (actual or improvised), singing, humming, electronically or by any means producing or reproducing a rhythmic melodic form.

Eliot had this stupid fascination with music—and an even greater fascination with the violin their father had given him.

In truth, though, Eliot and his music had done some amazing things. Magical things. Terrible things. But it was unpredictable, and that scared Fiona.

"Your music . . . ," Audrey said.

She opened her mouth to say more, but for some reason Audrey hesitated, as if she was actually weighing the issues. Fiona had never seen her perseverate over anything in her life. Audrey always knew her mind—and she never changed it once made.

"We shall lift this rule as well," Audrey finally said. "Play you must. I sense it is in your blood. But go slowly, Eliot, for you play with fire."

"Yes, Mother." Eliot eased back into his seat. "Thank you."

So he was calling her Mother now? How annoying.

But maybe it was okay as long as he kept his mouth shut about the other rules. Even Eliot had to know better than to push their luck further. Two rules lifted in one day was real progress.

"Ah!" Audrey brightened. "I'd almost forgotten." She opened her briefcase and retrieved a sheaf of legal-sized pages.

She set the inch-thick stack on the table and pushed it toward Fiona and Eliot.

Fiona grabbed it and pulled it away from her brother.

"The Council sent it this morning," Audrey told them. "Turn to page six. That is the only relevant piece you need concern yourself with."

Fiona flipped ahead.

She and Eliot read:

EDICTS GOVERNING NEW LEAGUE MEMBERS

1. New members must not under any circumstance, or by any means, convey, imply, or by means of not providing answers reveal the existence of the League of Immortals to non–League members.

2. With identical limitations as per Provision One, new members must not reveal their nonmortal status to mortals.

3. New members must not discuss the subjects of Provisions One and Two in public, where third parties may clandestinely eavesdrop, lip-read, or record conversations.

4. New members are accountable to these provisions/edicts and subject to penalties provided in Appendix D as sent forth by the Punishment and Enforcement Bureau circa 1878.

(continued on the next page . . .)

"I hope," Audrey said, "you two realized how seriously the League takes these matters." She retrieved the pages, straightened them, and returned them to her briefcase.

"Wait . . . ," Fiona said. The words she had read felt like concrete poured around her . . . slowly but inexorably solidifying. "So we're in the League of Immortals, and for the first time special and different—but we can't tell anyone who we are?"

"Of course you can tell people who you are," Audrey said. The warmth she had had in her voice earlier evaporated. "You will, naturally, say that you are Fiona and Eliot Post. That should be enough for anyone—including yourselves."

A spark of resentment fanned to life in Fiona. More lies? That's what the League was expecting from them?

"Fine," Fiona muttered. "Whatever." She stood and turned to her brother. "Come on. We better go."

Although Fiona now stood while her mother remained sitting, Audrey still managed to make it feel like she was looking down at her.

Fiona hated that imperial look.

So she had finally called her Mother . . . at least, in her mind.

But Audrey would never be the kind of mother who showed her how to put makeup on, or helped her pick out clothes, or had that heartfelt talk about the pleasures and perils of boys.

No. Fiona knew *exactly* what kind of mother Audrey was: the kind she read about in Shakespeare's plays—mothers who plotted and schemed and murdered and then compulsively washed their hands.

"Sit, young lady," Audrey told her. "We are not done."

The spark of resentment in Fiona chilled. She obediently sank into her seat.

"You are correct," Audrey told them. "There is a need to start school with all due haste, but you also need these materials if you are to have any chance of success . . . success, I might add, which the League considers *mandatory*."

Fiona shot Eliot a look. He shrugged, and his forehead wrinkled at this new development.

If they didn't do well at school, the Immortals would do what? Kick them out of the League? Something worse? Maybe. The League considered passing and failing tests a life-or-death matter. If they'd failed its three heroic trials, the League would have killed her and Eliot.

But come on—they were *in* the League now, considered an official part of the family. They didn't have to constantly prove themselves. Did they?

Audrey withdrew a blue envelope from her briefcase and slid it to them.

The envelope had a bar code sticker and a bewildering collection of stamps from Greece, Italy, Russia, places Fiona did not recognize, and finally the United States. It was addressed to "Master Eliot Zachariah Post and the Lady Fiona Paige Post" at their new San Francisco address.

And it had been opened.

As if her mother anticipated Fiona's objections, she said, "I filled out all the forms to save time. There is a list of rules and regulations, which you may read after the entrance and placement exams today." Audrey pinned the envelope with a stare. "Most important, however, there is a map—which you require immediately."

Fiona pulled out the first page.

The impressive Paxington Institute crest—a heraldic device with shield, helmet, and sword; a sleeping dragon; snarling wolf head; winged chevron; and gold scarab—dominated the scrollwork of a letterhead. Fiona's eyes gravitated to the boldface portion of the letter:

> *All students must be at Bristlecone Hall before 10:00 a.m., September 22, for placement examinations or their enrollment at Paxington will be forfeited.*

Fiona and Eliot wheeled around. Their grandfather clock sat in the corner. It read a quarter until nine.

"Where is Paxington?" Eliot asked, sounding embarrassed he didn't know.

Fiona riffled through the envelope, found the map, and pulled it out. She unfolded heavy cotton paper and saw exacting details of streets and landmarks like Presidio Park, Chinatown, and Fisherman's Wharf. The edges of the map were yellowed with age.

She found the Paxington Institute address as well as these helpful directions:

> The main entrance to the San Francisco Paxington campus is conveniently located at the intersection of Chestnut and Lombard Streets.

They glanced back at the map. Chestnut and Lombard were only a few blocks away.

"Only a fifteen-minute walk," Eliot said.

"I can see that," Fiona replied.

Something was wrong about this. She ran her fingertips over the map. The rough cotton fibers had a texture that felt like woven canvas. It made her skin itch.

Of course there was something wrong. You'd have thought they might for once treat her and Eliot like adults. Instead of outgrowing their household rules, though, they still had 104 old rules *plus* new League edicts to follow (along with some veiled threats if they failed) *and* a bunch of Paxington regulations to worry about.

Audrey stood and told them, "You must be on your way. Now. You will require every minute." Her face was unreadable.

Cecilia then emerged from the kitchen, a paper lunch sack in either hand. To Fiona's utter embarrassment, their names had been written on the outside as if they were little kids.

Cee shook the bags. "Special lunches today," she said, and smiled, "for my special darlings." She gave one to

Fiona and then Eliot, and hugged them both. "You'll do fine today." Her face darkened, and she whispered, "Remember to work *with* each other. You're far stronger together." Cecilia stood back and beamed at them. "Their first day of—"

"Which will be their last," Audrey told her, "if they delay."

"Oh, yes, silly me." Cecilia backed away.

"Thanks, Cee," Fiona said.

"Thanks," Eliot said.

She and Eliot moved to Audrey and gave her a kiss on the cheek. To Fiona, this felt like one of her morning chores, like brushing her teeth or taking out the trash.

Eliot ran down the hall.

Fiona sprinted after him and got ahead, tramping down the spiral staircase first, and halted at the front door. "Too slow again," she told him.

The front door was redwood and had four stained glass windows depicting a rose-hedge maze, a meander of river, a field of grapevines and harvesters, and a coastline with churning waves. A million colors sparkled on the tiled floor.[3]

Fiona loved this door and paused to admire it.

"We'd better go," Eliot whispered. "There's something weird about this Paxington map deal."

---

3. The Door of Four Paths and the Post residence were some of the few structures to miraculously survive the devastation that flattened the San Francisco peninsula in the War of Last Judgment. The four windows depict (or some claim are) doorways to the Middle Realms. This artifact from the Fifth Celestial Age continues to undergo intense and cautious study. For humanity, these windows remain symbols of mystery, wonder, and hope. *Gods of the First and Twenty-first Century, Volume 11, The Post Family Mythology.* Zypheron Press Ltd., Eighth Edition.

"I know," Fiona said. "I feel it, too."

She glanced back up the stairwell, hoping to see Audrey looking down, maybe with the tiniest farewell wave.

But her mother wasn't there . . . only shadows.

2

꒦

CIRCLES OF POWER AND REGRET

Audrey watched from the second-story window as the children walked down the street. They paused at the intersection and looked both ways before crossing. She reached up and touched the glass.

Always so careful. Good for them. The world was a dangerous place, and it was wise to look before one leaped. But sometimes being cautious was bad. Wait too long to cross the road, and one might be hit from behind by a bus careening out of control down the sidewalk.

She withdrew her hand, returned to the dining table, and sat.

"We must talk," Cecilia whispered to her. "The children—"

Audrey held up one finger. "Tea first, Cecilia. And bring the Towers game. I fear the time will crawl today without some distraction."

Cecilia obediently nodded and backed into the kitchen.

Boiling water for tea. The old woman hopefully could manage that.

Audrey nibbled on a piece of curled burnt bacon and reminded herself to make a list of all the restaurants nearby that delivered breakfast, lunch, and dinner. There was no need anymore to pretend they did not have the money for such "luxuries" as edible food.

Cecilia returned with a tea service tray and a rolled-up piece of leather.

Indeed, there was no need anymore to pretend *many* things.

Cecilia smiled nervously. "You have that look on your face"—she poured hot water into a teapot with spiderweb patterns etched into its white glaze—"the look where people go missing."

Odors of chamomile, mint, and mandrake wafted across the table.

"I was just thinking that there are advantages to having some things cut." Audrey sighed. "Set up the game and ask no more foolish questions."

Cecilia paled. She unrolled the leather mat upon the table and then removed the game cubes from their pouch.

Long ago, Audrey had had to sever herself from a collection of feelings and instincts that some might call motherhood. She'd left only one connection: the instinct to protect.

Did she still love her children? Was there some vestige of a desire to give them the best of everything? Where was the urge to hold them and soothe away their fears when they had nightmares? Or were these things forever lost to her?

It had to be that way, though. Otherwise, she would not have had the strength to do what was best for them all.

Audrey shifted her focus to the game. It was a study on the forms of combat, on strategies and death, a metaphor on the families and their never-ending politics. They called the game Towers.[4]

Audrey smoothed the rumpled leather mat and ran her fingers over the lines that radiated from the center, around the circles that divided the space into four tiers. Slaves (or their modern equivalent, Pawns) sat on the outer edge. Warriors took the second tier. Princes collected near the nexus of power on the third tier. The Master sat in the center space. Rings about rings. Rings of power and love and deception and regret.

She and Cecilia divided the stone cubes and took alternating turns, selecting their starting positions along their respective inner areas.

Much of the game was decided by this deceptively simple planning stage. Good players could tell how their game would end from such opening moves. One could set up near an opponent's boundary, preparing for an aggressive rush. Or they could set up in the back regions and strategize to take the center—a longer game of dominance and subtlety.

---

4. Fragments of one Towers set were found in the Neolithic hunter-gatherer settlement, Göbekli Tepe (southeast Turkey c. 9000 B.C.E.). This makes Towers the oldest (nontrivial) game, predating Chinese Go and Egyptian Senet by more than four thousand years. A Towers board is circular. Lines radiate outward to make thirty-two spaces of alternating color on the circumference, a second tier closer of sixteen spaces, a third tier with eight spaces, and a single circular space in the center. Placed on the board are sixteen white cubes and sixteen black. A simple checkers mechanism was assumed, but in 1753, a set was discovered in Pompeii preserved *in the middle* of a game. Cubes were stacked into towers (of increasing size) on the inner circles, while others remained as single stones, indicating a complexity of rules that experts agree no Neolithic hunter-gathers could have developed. *Gods of the First and Twenty-first Century, Volume 1, Earliest Myths.*

Like the twins. How things went today at school would very much affect their endgame.

Cecilia set up on Audrey's boundary. In response, Audrey placed only a few weak defenders to counter her and concentrated her efforts on the longer back-region game.

Cee immediately took one of Audrey's border guards. "I am worried about their father," she said, a smug smile appearing on her face as she removed Audrey's piece.

"There has been no word from him," Audrey replied.

"Exactly!" Cee said. "It can mean only one thing: He's plotting something."

Audrey's answer to this obvious statement was silence.

She countered Cecilia's move by advancing a stone from her first circle to the second, blocking Cee's clumsy advance.

"We should tell the children," Cecilia said. "Tell them everything." She poured Audrey and herself cups of tea. Steam curled around the old woman like living tendrils. "We should prepare them for the coming violence."

"No."

"But this is not like the last time, when their ignorance protected them."

"Their ignorance serves a purpose still," Audrey told her. "They have lessons to learn. The entire truth would only distract them."

"But they are so smart." Cecilia moved another piece along her opposite border, poised to attack.

Audrey moved another cube onto her second tier, stacking it with the first to make a low Tower.

Cecilia frowned at this, realizing her error. She moved

one of her own cubes to the second tier. Too late, however, to be an effective counter.

"'Smart' will help them only so much," Audrey said. "Better they learn how to be *ruthless*. They must be pushed to the brink, broken, and then remolded. It is the only way they have a chance of surviving."

"And the place for this is Paxington? That so-called Headmistress, Miss Westin. We will be lucky if she does not kill them first."

"Westin is not the threat she once was to children," Audrey told her. She toppled her fledgling Tower, casting its pieces into Cecilia's territory, capturing two of her cubes. "Besides, I have spoken with her. All is arranged."

"Oh, I see," Cecilia said, now ignoring the game. "Miss Westin and Paxington are vastly reformed since the old days, eh? Did you know that seventeen children were so severely injured last year that they could not continue? That there were five fatalities?"

"Of course," Audrey replied. "I believe that's the point."

Cecilia sipped her tea. "That is not the only danger. The students, they are from the families, ours, theirs, all the other great ones, mortal and immortal—the social elite and privileged few." She huffed. "Do you know what they will do to our poor little lambs?"

"They will devour them," Audrey told her, "if Eliot and Fiona fail to grow."

Cecilia glowered at Audrey. Without looking at the board, she moved another cube onto the second tier.

Audrey raised an eyebrow. Interesting. In three moves, Cecilia would capture the entire second ring. The old witch apparently had some spark left to her.

"You think me a monster," Audrey replied. "But you've forgotten the real monsters in our world: horrors with bat wings and serpent tongues, nightmares made real." She cocked her head, hearing the heartbeat and breath she'd been waiting for all morning. "Especially the monsters with sharp smiles and large ears 'the better to hear with.'"

Audrey turned to face the stairwell. "Come in, Old Wolf. The door is open to you."

Beneath them came the sound of the door's locks clicking open, the knob turning, and whisper-silent footfalls.

Faint gray shadows crisscrossed the spiral of stairs as a figure came up.

His smile was the first thing she saw, like some hybrid Cheshire cat and great white shark making a grand entrance. Henry Mimes gave her a short bow and then gave one to Cecilia as well. He was dressed for walking today: gray slacks, sensible sneakers, a black turtleneck, and a baseball cap that framed his silver hair.

Dangerously handsome and dangerously deceptive.

And yet . . . Audrey could not help but smile back at the fool, if only a little.

"What do you want, Henry?" Audrey said. "Your visits are never merely to exchange pleasantries."

"It could be that way . . . if you desired, my Queen of Swords." Henry looked about the room. "How quaint. I see you still have my grandfather clock in good repair." His gaze caught the picture window and its view of the bay and the Golden Gate Bridge. "A lovely location. I approve."

Cecilia, stone-faced, poured a cup of tea for Henry and offered it to him.

He smiled, accepted her gift . . . but paused as the vapors reached his nose. "Thank you, dear witch of the Isle Eea." He set the cup back on the table. "I think we'll pass on your poison this morning."

Cecilia wisely said nothing.

"You're in an unusually good mood," Audrey said.

"Am I not always?" His attention drifted to the game of Towers. "But you're right, today is special: my favorite nephew and niece's first day of high school. So many plots and devices afoot. It makes for a delectable mix."

"So many words," Cecilia hissed, "and yet he says so little."

Henry's smile cooled a few degrees, but his gaze did not lift from the board. "You know, old woman, that you can win in six turns? Here." He reached over and slid two cubes at once to flank Audrey's collapsed tower.

"That's not a legitimate move," Cecilia told him.

"It is," Henry said. "Just one that you, in your too-long years, have failed to learn. Or perhaps senility has settled upon your once-keen mind?"

Audrey saw that her captured pieces could be used to build additional Towers on Cecilia's side in three moves—and her own border defenses after that would be insufficient. While she could still get to the center, Henry's new strategy had her losing her entire back-court . . . and then the game.

She locked eyes with him. There was no more emotion or additional truths, however, behind his sparkling empty eyes.

"One must practice to keep one's defenses sharpened, no?" he asked.

"The Council?"

"Meeting today," Henry replied. "They require our presence. I thought that I would offer you a ride."

"Always and never the gentleman," Audrey said, and stood. "I accept your offer."

"Splendid," Henry cooed. He turned to Cecilia, and

his slender hand reached out to caress her face. Cecilia recoiled before this gesture. "Ah, I would bring you as well, my lovely," he said, "but there are some on the Council who would love to part your head from your shoulders should you cross their path."

Cecilia gripped a butter knife.

Henry spared a glance at its edge. "Perhaps another time you and I will dance." He moved to the stairs. "Today, regrettably, we have business to attend to: The Council wishes to discuss its newest members, and provided they are allowed to live . . . we shall discuss how to avert the end of the world."

Audrey gathered her courage and followed. "I expected no less."

3

ENTRANCE EXAM

Eliot had this creepy feeling he and Fiona were being watched. Fog and shafts of sunlight swirled around them on the sidewalk. He glanced up at their new house.

He liked it. It wasn't "home." That had been their apartment in Del Sombra. This place, though, made up for it by at least having more than one bathroom.

It was a modern Victorian squished on all sides so it towered three stories tall on their lot. The trim was green and gold geometric art deco lines. Three scalloped balconies cupped the sides of the house like bracket mushrooms. A gold solar system weather vane topped the highest spire. It was an odd melding of styles . . . but it somehow worked, like something a mad genius architect might have sketched.

Every building was tall and quirky on their street—stacked at least three stories tall. Most had been built with so little room, they actually touched their neighbors. Cee said it was the high cost of real estate that made every home tiny and built this way.

That feeling of being watched, however, was still there. Eliot squinted, but the windows of his house were solid reflections of sky.

Fiona glanced around, too, perhaps sensing the same unease he felt.

"Are you ready?" she asked.

"Hang on a sec." Eliot tightened the strap of his canvas backpack. Inside were pencils, notebooks, Cee's lunch, and a battered violin case (sticking slightly out of the top of the pack), which contained his most prized possession: the violin Lady Dawn. He shifted his shoulders inside his too-big Paxington jacket. No luck there—it still looked all wrong. "Okay," he told her. "Let's go."

Fiona unfolded their map, got oriented, and then pointed. "That way to Lombard Street." She marched ahead and Eliot followed. She was in her figure-it-out mode, and nothing got in Fiona's way when she was like that.

For several blocks they tromped in silence and then turned onto Lombard.

A nonstop stream of cars and trucks rolled by. Eliot and Fiona took a step back. The scents of coffee and freshly baked bread drifted with the odors of exhaust. People queued in line for coffee from latte carts.

"All we have to do is follow this street west," she told him. "That'll get us there." She scrutinized the map but looked unconvinced.

"What's the matter?" he asked.

"Nothing."

Eliot knew it was *something*, but before he could get it out of his sister, she started walking.

Why did she always do that? Leave him behind, thinking she got to lead. Eliot had half a mind to go his own way . . . but then, Fiona might get lost and never find the place by herself.

So he followed. For her sake.

One day, though, she was going to find out just how much she needed him.

They passed shoe stores and a Taco Bell and one store that sold nothing but globes and maps. Fiona paused to admire a massive world that levitated magnetically on its pedestal. She checked the building's street number and then compared it to the address on their welcome letter.

"This is the right direction," she said. "We should almost be there."

Lombard veered southwest. The street narrowed and filled with houses and apartments. Eliot didn't see anything that looked like a school.

They walked another entire block—passing the address where Paxington should have been—the last two digits of the closest number jumped from 16 to 22.

"You're reading that map wrong," Eliot told her.

"I'm not," she replied.

Eliot then did the one thing he had vowed he wouldn't do this morning. He dug into his pack, found a slender case, and pulled it out. Inside were his new glasses. The silver wire rims made him look like an ultra-dork when he wore them.

"Let me try," he said.

Fiona glanced back down the street, confused. "Fine." She handed him the map and letter.

He donned his glasses, cringing as he did so, but the pages came into focus. He checked the Paxington address, and then their map.

"Look," he told Fiona, "it says it's at the intersection of Lombard and Chestnut Streets. We've checked Lombard. We should go down Chestnut instead."

Fiona examined the map. "It's only one block north of here." She almost looked impressed with this idea, but then added: "Not bad . . . for an *Architeuthis dux*."

Eliot ground his teeth at this simultaneous compliment and insult. *Architeuthis dux* was the scientific name for the giant squid. Its eye was one of the largest in the animal kingdom—the size of a volleyball—and could spot prey in the murkiest ocean depths. Her commentary on his new glasses.

As he mulled over the appropriate counterinsult, Fiona grabbed the map and letter and flounced down a side street. "Come on," she called back. "Don't sulk . . . it was a good idea."

Eliot removed his glasses, placed them back in their case, and dashed after her.

They emerged on Chestnut Street with its quaint pastel and stucco houses and apartments jam-packed together, every parking spot filled, and even more people on the sidewalks—all of whom seemed to be very much in a hurry to get to work, or jogging as fast as they could, or delivering very important-looking packages.

. . . or like them, just trying to get school.

Eliot spotted a navy blue wool jacket, khaki slacks, and a flash of gold threads shimmering from an embroidered Paxington crest.

Another student.

Eliot pointed to this boy on the opposite side of the street. "Let's follow him."

Fiona nodded, and they raced alongside, shadowing the other student until they came to a crosswalk. The light was red. The other boy crossed; they had to wait.

Eliot watched the traffic. There was a break coming. They could sprint across the street, but technically, that was against the law—jaywalking—and something Audrey would definitely have disapproved of.

He thought, however, she'd disapprove *more* of them being late for their first day of school.

Eliot started to cross.

"You can't do that!" Fiona shouted after him—but nonetheless she followed.

A truck pulled out of a driveway and accelerated toward them.

Eliot and Fiona sprinted.

The truck blared its horn.

They jumped together onto the sidewalk. A whirlwind of dust and fumes and papers swirled around them.

"That was stupid," she hissed.

"There he is!" Eliot said, ignoring her, and ran after the boy from Paxington.

The student must have heard him, because he turned. The boy was older, eighteen maybe, two heads taller than Eliot, and he had a faint mustache. His dark hair was long and wavy and combed back. He was deeply tanned and muscular. He smiled at them.

Eliot found himself smiling back. A friendly face was the last thing he expected today, but he was glad to find one.

The boy held out his hand for Eliot to shake and

asked, "Paxington? Transfer students?" His voice was embroidered with a rich Italian accent.

"Yes," Eliot replied. "And no."

Up close, Eliot noticed the boy's uniform was different from theirs. The fabric was smoother and of a more luxuriant texture. It looked like it had been custom tailored.

Fiona and Eliot shifted uncomfortably in their too-baggy and too-tight uniforms.

The boy gave Fiona a slight bow. "You look like you might need some help. Allow me to introduce myself. I am from the family Scalagari. My given name is Dante."

"It's great to meet you. I'm Eliot. Eliot Post. And this is my sister—"

"Fiona." She tried to smile, but it wavered and failed. "We were beginning to worry that we had the wrong street."

"Can you help us find the school?" Eliot asked.

Dante Scalagari's smile faded. "Ah, I see. You must forgive me. I did not know you were freshmen. You both look . . . well, take no offense, but you look like you've seen more of the world than our typical freshman."

"Yeah, I guess so," Eliot said.

Fiona cleared her throat and glanced at the sidewalk. "If you don't mind very much . . . we have to get to the placement exams before the time runs out."

Dante held out his hands in an apologetic gesture. "Believe me," he said, "I've nothing against you. In fact, you have my deepest sympathies. But, alas, I cannot show you the way."

"What?" Eliot said. "Why!"

Dante's hands clasped and his fingers interlaced.

"Tradition," he said. "Rules. And because I'm late for school myself. Perhaps I will see you again on campus."

"If you just point us in the right direction," Fiona said, and started to unfold their map.

Eliot leaned closer and traced their route, explaining, "We tried following Lombard, but that didn't . . ."

He glanced up.

Eliot looked back and forth along the sidewalk. There was no trace of Dante Scalagari.

"Impossible," Fiona breathed. Her head snapped sideways. "Wait, there's another student."

Eliot saw them as well. A girl this time; he caught just a glimpse of platinum curls over the Paxington navy blue blazer—as she turned a corner, entered the shadows, and disappeared from view.

Fiona sighed. She looked over the map again. "Well, with two students so close, the school has to be nearby. Let's go this way."

They followed the street numbers as they increased, and once more passed where Paxington *should have* been—but clearly wasn't.

Fiona clutched the map, crinkling its edges. "What are we doing wrong?"

Eliot leaned closer and examined the map. "The directions said it was at the intersection of Lombard and Chestnut?" He followed those two roads with his fingers. "That can't be right. They must mean Richardson Avenue. That cuts across both."

"Not Richardson," Fiona told him. "It specifically said the intersection of Lombard and Chestnut."

"I remember what it said," Eliot answered, anger creeping into his voice. "I'm not an idiot. I'm saying that's impossible because they run parallel. They *never* cross."

Fiona checked, and then double-checked this.

"Give me the map." Eliot gently took hold of one corner. "I'll puzzle it out."

Fiona refused to release her grip. She pulled away. "They *have* to cross somewhere."

Eliot didn't let go either. The map snapped taut between them. He pulled hard.

Fiona yanked the map, too.

The yellowed parchment tore down the middle . . . almost all the way through.

Eliot stared at the ruined map, remembering how Cee had told them to work together. And here they were: they hadn't found Paxington, let alone faced the placement exams, and were already fighting each other.

He glared at his sister.

She glared back at him. "Great," she said. "Like we don't have enough trouble already."

"Thanks to you," Eliot said. "Just because you're a 'goddess' now doesn't mean you know everything . . . or even anything."

Fiona tilted her chin up and tried to look "down" at him the way Audrey could. It didn't work.

"At least *now* you know how to make two parallel lines meet," Eliot told her.

"What do you mean?"

Eliot snorted. "It's easy, but useless, really." He crossed one of the map's torn flaps so Lombard and Chestnut Streets, once parallel, angled toward each other.

Static electricity raced up his fingertips, growing stronger as he brought the pieces of the map together.

Fiona guided the other part of the map toward his. "I've felt something like this before," she whispered.

The two portions of the map wavered as if magnetically attracted and then repulsed . . . and then the two sides snapped together.

Lombard and Chestnut crossed—at least on paper.

Fiona ran her fingers over the parchment. "This feels like that spot in the Valley of the New Year where there was a hidden exit. A spot where space *folded*."

"Like there's an extra space or a doorway"—Eliot pointed to the spot where the two streets intersected—"here?"

"We passed that spot and didn't see anything," she said.

"But did we *really* look?"

They stared at the map. The "intersection" was a block and a half away.

Fiona crumpled the outer edges of the map, and they both ran.

They dodged people on the sidewalk; Eliot careened off a trash can, stumbled, but kept going. He caught glimpses of other Paxington students, but didn't bother to ask for help. There was no time left.

They sprinted toward the address where Paxington was supposed to be, where the lines crossed on the map.

It looked like the same place they had walked by earlier . . . but it *felt* different.

That static electricity sensation was here.

He slowed and stopped.

So did Fiona.

They looked for something out of the ordinary. There was only a wall made of roughened granite blocks.

Eliot ran his hand over the surface.

It was just rock . . . but there *was* something else, faint at first, and then stronger. Deep inside the stone there was a vibration, almost like he was touching the strings of his violin.

Fiona felt the wall with both her hands. "It's like threads," she whispered.

"Like music," he said.

He spied a minuscule crack in the stone, and as he touched its edges, there was a pause in the music.

Fiona found the spot as well.

Eliot stared at the crack and found that when he looked at it from a particular angle—*an angle that hadn't been there before*—the crack tilted and expanded and was really a *four*-dimensional corner.

Disorientation washed over him as this new space revealed itself. The sensation was like staring at one of those crazy M. C. Escher drawings: Everything appeared normal, until suddenly you saw an extra dimension tilting sideways.

Eliot and Fiona stepped around this new corner and found themselves—

—on a cobblestone boulevard running *perpendicular* to the main street.

It wasn't as if this new passage were hidden. It opened quite plainly onto the main street behind them.

Eliot waved to a man as he rushed past on the sidewalk. "Hey, mister," he called.

The man ignored him.

Apparently no one on the outside could sense this place, unless they knew exactly what they were looking for.[5]

---

5. In the late twentieth and early twenty-first centuries, inspectors from the State, Fire, and School Accreditation Boards easily found the Main Gate entrance of the Paxington Institute, but when reporters or tourists attempted to locate the entrance, they failed. This might simply be the nature of San Francisco's convoluted street geometry. In old satellite images, the original Paxington campus does appear exactly where school officials claim (adjacent Presidio Park). Similar modern accounts, however, of the school's "selectively appearing entrance" have been claimed of the new Paxington Institute on the San Francisco Archipelago. Inquiries made to the Institute result in a detailed set of directions . . . which ultimately prove use-

There were a dozen stores on this in-between street: antique and curio shops, a few high-end fashion boutiques, a Chinese noodle house, and a café on the corner, where older Paxington students sat at canopy-covered tables. Farther down the boulevard, brick walls rose along the sides, weathered and ivy-covered, which ended a half block away at an intricate wrought iron gate.

Beyond those gates were majestic cathedral-like buildings stained black with age, structures with Greek columns that rose like a forest of marble, and wavering in and out of the ever-present Bay Area fog lorded a clock tower glinting with hints of gold filigree.

"It's amazing," Eliot said.

"Yeah. . . ." Fiona immediately sobered. "But the time!" She grabbed his hand and pulled him along.

Eliot shook off his wonderment and ran with her.

As they neared the gate, Eliot saw that it was shut. Had they let everyone inside already and locked the place up?

A man with a stern look on his face stepped out of the gatehouse. He wore a navy blue suit with an embroidered Paxington crest. His blond hair was buzzcut, and his beard was trimmed square, save the two braids that dangled from his chin.

He towered over Eliot and Fiona, but more impressive than his height was his girth. It would've taken three muscular men standing side by side to occupy the same space where he stood. His biceps flexed and stretched taut the fabric of his jacket.

He raised a clipboard and made two checks. "Master

Eliot Post," he muttered, "and the Lady Fiona Post. Good morning."

"Yes, sir." Eliot panted. "Good morning. Sorry." He gave this man a short bow, unsure what the protocol was, but very sure that he deserved respect.

Fiona curtsied.

"Congratulations on passing the entrance exam," the man said.

"Entrance exam?" Eliot echoed.

"A test to see if you have a spark. You'd be surprised how many potential freshmen wander just outside this street, sometimes for days, never giving up, but never having what it takes to get inside, either. So sad."

The man's iron stance relaxed a notch. "I am Harlan Dells," he said. "Head of security at Paxington. Mind you two break no rules while on school grounds or you will answer to me."

Eliot swallowed.

Harlan Dells glared at Eliot's backpack.

Eliot felt his violin case shift inside. His hand tingled where Lady Dawn's snapped string had cut and infected him . . . apparently not so healed as he had thought.

Harlan Dells turned and opened the gate.

Something about the man was familiar. It was like when they had met Uncle Henry; Eliot felt an instinctual fear and some déjà vu. He sensed that Mr. Dells was related in *some* way. He was an Immortal.

Mr. Dells faced them. "I can hear the grass grow on the other side of the world. I can see the farthest shore, the most distant star . . . and I can be in more than one place at a time, so I can easily spot and catch two troublemakers. Understand?"

"Yes, sir," Eliot and Fiona said together.

"Good." Mr. Dells pointed past the gates—over manicured lawns and marble fountains, across the courtyard to the Clock Tower and a domed building next to it. "Bristlecone Hall," he told them. "That's where your placement exams are this morning."

The minute hand of the tower clock ticked into the straight-up position, and bells tolled.

"I suggest," Mr. Dells said, "that you run for it."

They did.

4

WHAT WE DO BEST

Louis Piper, often called the Prince of Darkness, Lucifer, or the Morning Star, mused on the nature of time . . . how when one doted upon a beautiful woman, a moment stretched into days . . . or like now, when one waited for his cousins to deliberate on their endless scheming—it took an eternity.

Louis shifted on the vinyl couch.

This waiting room was devoid of comfort. Windowless, the only ornamentation on the water-stained walls was a USA AS SEEN FROM LAS VEGAS poster. The odor of urinal cake wafted from the adjacent restroom.

Aside from the door marked EXIT, the only other egress was the door leading to the recently relocated Las Vegas Boardroom.

"They should've called me in already," he told Amberflaxus. "Something is wrong."

Next to him on the couch, his cat ceased licking its iridescent black fur and blinked.

"Yes, yes, I know," Louis replied. "One cannot go from King of the Panhandlers to Chairman of the Board in a single season, can one?"

Louis reached to stroke Amberflaxus.

The cat, lightning quick, batted his hand away and gave a look of offense.

"No? You're saying what right do I have to make such claims? I, who have wandered homeless and clueless as a mortal for sixteen years, his power severed and heart ripped asunder by the woman he loved?"

Had he really loved? Louis had forgotten. Perhaps it was just a bad dream.

His cat returned to licking himself.

Louis leaned closer. "You make perfect sense. Consider, though, my friend, that in the span of a few days, I have regained my Infernal status, killed our loathsome cousin Beelzebub, and absorbed his power. What stops me from marching in there and *demanding* a seat on the Board?"

Amberflaxus tore into the vinyl couch—shredding wildly as if the plastic were alive.

His sentiments were obvious: Louis was a fool.

Any of Louis's relations had the power to slay hero or demon. But without land, Louis was a pale imitation of a *real* Infernal. Land made them what they were.

The door to the Boardroom eased open.

No one emerged to invite Louis in, a sign of his lower-than-dirt status. So be it.

He stood, brushed cat hair from his charcoal gray suit, and straightened his bloodred tie.

Amberflaxus bit into the couch's stuffing, shaking nubs of fluff.

"Wait here," he told the animal.

Louis turned, donned his armored smile, and entered.

The Boardroom had been a private gambling den during Prohibition. Six billiard lamps hung from the rafters, making cones of dust-filled light. On the far wall hung a gigantic computer screen showing the local news coverage of the Babylon Garden Hotel and Casino as preparations were made to demolish the place in one well-engineered implosion. That was Beelzebub's nightclub, the last of his old bones being scattered in a final act of well-deserved degradation.

In the center of the room was a craps table padded with green felt, its lines and numbers worn smooth with age where bets were placed with chips, gold coins, or souls.

About the table stood the Infernal Board of Directors.

Louis bowed without taking his eyes off any of them.

Sealiah turned to face Louis. She stood at the foot of the table. She wore an evening gown of opal-flecked orchids and clinging copper vines that wrapped her sinuous curves for a predictable effect upon his libido. Her hair flashed red gold, her sharp smile, pure white, and her eyes, slits of emerald.

"We welcome the glorious Morning Star," Sealiah told him (although from her icy tone, Louis was sure *welcome* was the last thing she meant).

"Greetings to you, Cousin, Queen of Poppies and Mistress of the Many-Colored Jungles."

Louis stared past her to the head of the table at the Board's new Chairman, Ashmed, the Master Architect of Evil.

Ashmed was the most careful among their kind. His friends remained loyal . . . and those who did not lived short lives. The Chairman was all business—crew-cut hair, clean shaved, and in a black business suit.

"Welcome, Louis." Ashmed puffed on a Sancho Panza Belicosos cigar and blew a trail of serpentine smoke. "Kind of you to appear on short notice."

"Anything for the Board," Louis replied.

Lev, called Leviathan by some, the Master of the Endless Abyssal Seas, stood on Ashmed's right. A hundred strands of Mardi Gras beads coiled about his throat, which almost covered his straining-to-the-bursting-point wife-beater tank top. His corpulence matched his endless strength.

"Really?" Lev asked, and his beady eyes widened. "If you'd do 'anything'—then cut off your right arm. You owe me for that business in Mozambique."

Lev was too powerful to insult directly, but thankfully his intellect was as dull as his doughy features.

"Almost anything for you, Cousin, would I not do," Louis told him.

Lev's fat forehead crinkled as he puzzled this grammatical knot.

The doors behind Louis shut . . . which was not a good sign.

"Please, Lev," a girl whispered, "do not play with your food."

Louis spied a slender form standing between Sealiah and Leviathan.

"Abigail," Louis cooed. "I did not see you." He bowed to her. "A thousand apologies. Destroy everything you touch."

"Lies and salutations to you, dear Cousin," Abby replied.

She was so quiet, so lithe—her delicate childlike

features artfully covered in translucent gauze and seed pearls—so enticing that Louis could *almost* forget she was the Destroyer, Handmaiden of Armageddon, and Mistress of the Palace of Abomination.

However, those who underestimated Abby found their guts trailing from their torsos.

Abby held a locust in the palm of her white hand. It shivered and made the most unpleasant buzzing sound imaginable. She stroked the insect and it calmed. "Did you hear? Oz has retired, poor thing. Allow me to introduce our newest Board member." She tilted her chin to the other side of the table.

Oz had crossed Lev and Abby earlier this year. He was lucky to have escaped with most of his skin intact, a tribute to his eel slipperiness.

Louis peered into the shadows and saw a silhouette on the other side of the table, one he had failed to detect earlier . . . which, when you considered that all Infernals lived, breathed, and were part darkness themselves, made this a masterwork of deception indeed.

"Mephistopheles," Louis said.

Naturally, Louis was disappointed. He had hoped the Board brought him here to offer *him* a seat.

But why should they? He was dirt, worthless and landless, having the barest scraps of power to his name. Only his reputation for being the Great Liar enabled him to hold his head high among them.

Yet why Mephistopheles? Irritation prickled Louis. After his scandalous behavior at the end of the Dark Ages with that fop Dr. Faustus—and then the operas— all the fame and the paparazzi. This sparked a hundred imitators trying to summon "the Devil" to sell their souls for trinkets. It had been a public relations nightmare.

Mephistopheles had retired, eschewing his family, claiming he had to strengthen his lands and borders.

Sulking, Louis called it.

Or could the rumors have been true? That he actually enjoyed the company of mortals . . . perhaps enjoyed them too much? Louis's smile faltered a split second. If that were the case, if he had fallen in love, had his heart broken as Louis had, he deserved pity.

"So good to . . . well . . . not see you, Lord of the House of Umbra, Ruler of the Hysterical Kingdom, and Prince of the Mirrored City," Louis told the darkness.

"Toy not with me, Louis," Mephistopheles rumbled. A taloned hand extended from the shadows and rested upon the table's railing, claws dimpling the green felt.

Sealiah cleared her throat. "Gentlemen, let us avoid tearing Louis into bits before we're done with him, as tempting as that may be. We have business."

"Yes," Ashmed said, setting down his cigar. "The business of the twins. We have called you among us to serve as consultant. You're close to the boy?"

"And the girl," Louis added. "I am, after all, their father."

He put on a brave face, but inside, Louis was wounded. They had summoned him here for the children's sake? Yes, yes, *they* were important: the key to unraveling the neutrality treaty with the League of Immortals.

But could someone, just once, want him for his own sparkling self?

This was the problem with being a narcissist: No one appreciated you as much as you knew you deserved.

"How can I be of service today?" Louis asked.

"This Board's previous efforts position the children

on a knife's edge," Mephistopheles said from his shadows, and his hand chopped down onto the table for emphasis. "Half Immortal, half Infernal. We must bring them into our jurisdiction."

"Temptations backfired on us," Lev said. "Those chocolates, the Valley of the New Year. Who knew the kids could use them to their advantage so quickly?"

"I believe," Abby interrupted, "that Sealiah's seductress—this new Jezebel—had *some* success?"

Sealiah betrayed no emotion on her beautiful features. A sign of deception, to be certain.

"Jezebel's real influence has yet to be seen," she said.

"And Beelzebub's attempt to *force* a solution," Ashmed continued, "proved disastrous."

Indeed. Louis had been there when his darling Fiona had parted the head of the Lord of All That Flies from his body.

"We need a new deception to bring them into the family," Abby said. "And since your blood runs through their veins, Louis, we had hoped you had a suggestion."

There it was, the one shred of truth in this maneuvering: They *needed* him.

The universe spun around Louis. He, who was a second ago more common than dirt, was suddenly the golden key to the ambitions of the Infernal clans. This was his chance, but to do what? Place his only two children in danger to gain advantage and power? And land . . . one could not forget the land to be gained.

But Eliot was so talented, playing his Lady Dawn.

And Fiona was so beautiful and so strong, and she didn't even know it.

Poisonous fatherly concern coursed through his veins and muddled his thinking.

This weakness—the vestiges of Louis's human form,

no doubt—would destroy him if he allowed such a cancerous influence to run its full course.

Thankfully, rational thinking prevailed.

Louis was many things, perhaps even a father to his children, but he had *never* been a fool in the face of opportunity.

"Yes," Louis replied to the Board, "I know how this might be accomplished."

The shadow form of Mephistopheles chuckled, and the subsonic noise made Louis's teeth rattle.

"Doubt if you will," Louis said, "but I know their weakness: They have been brought up to be 'good' children."

They stared at him, rapt. Louis had them now.

"A good little boy and girl, with all the ingredients that lead to moral downfall, including the most important: *good intentions*."

Ashmed nodded, picked up his cigar, and puffed, greatly pleased with this.

"Go on," Abby said, her eyes sparkling.

"We require a theater of Shakespearean proportions to draw the twins closer . . . as they have proved themselves highly susceptible to familial drama."

"Shakes-whos-its?" Lev asked. "You lost me."

"Shakespeare: the basis for all those Mexican soap operas you so love, Cousin," Louis explained.

"How, specifically, would one engineer this 'drama'?" Sealiah asked.

"We shall do what we do best," Louis said, and spread his arms wide. He congratulated himself on a smooth transition to using *we* to refer to himself and the Board as partners on this venture. "We shall do it by fighting amongst ourselves. A war, just a little one, should do the trick."

Of course, he was telling them all this because wars

had their winners and losers . . . and where there were losers, there would be pieces of land and power for Louis to scavenge.

Ashmed's dark gaze was light-years distant. "A sanctioned Civil War could destroy many clans," he said. "Are these two children worth that?"

"It need not be a full Civil War," Sealiah said. "Two clans would suffice. Something intimate. With only two involved, the loss to us would be trivial—negligible after we reabsorb the power base of the loser. Naturally, the specifics of how to draw Eliot and Fiona into the conflict would be left up to the individuals with the most at stake."

Despite this coming from Sealiah, Louis liked the addendum to his plan. With only two factions involved, he would not have to personally risk doing any of the dirty work.

"The destruction, however, of even a single clan," Ashmed reminded them, "is still a considerable tactical liability, since we are on the eve of war with the Immortals."

Lev laughed. "Terrible for the loser. Which *wouldn't* be me. Sign me up."

"I, too, want the chance to play," Abby whispered. "It has been too long since we had such sport. I volunteer my clan to go to war." Her hand clutched her pet locust, and it squealed.

"As do I," Sealiah stated.

Mephistopheles hammered a fist upon the railing, and the entire table jumped. "Fools—we all want blood on our hands. I propose we dispense with the usual discussion and move directly either to violence or dice to settle this."

"Excellent motion," Ashmed said. "Do we have a second?"

Louis took a step back from the table, feeling gravity condense about the Board members. He weighed who would fight whom . . . and who would survive. Lev was powerful but slow. Abby was unstoppable but gullible. Sealiah was ever full of tricks. Ashmed, he had never seen fight. And Mephistopheles? Perhaps the most dangerous here, with his pitchfork of shadow smoke.

With one wrong twitch, Louis could be caught in the middle of the mayhem.

"I will second the motion," Sealiah breathed, "for dice."

Louis exhaled.

Sealiah rubbed her palms, and a die appeared: a Naga of Dharma.

The last few times Louis had seen one of the legendary dice, they had decided Charlemagne would become Emperor, that they'd test-fire Mount Krakatoa in the fifth, sixth, and seventeenth centuries, and that some utterly forgettable film would win the Academy Award.

It was a cube of scrimshawed ivory carved from the spine of the world serpent. Only five such dice existed. On the faces were etched six crows, five hands (each making its own rude gesture), four stars, three crossed swords, two prancing dogs, and a single head-eating-tail asp.

Ashmed called for a vote.

Ashmed raised his hand—as did Sealiah and, curiously, even Mephistopheles. Abby and Lev did not.

This shocked Louis. Usually there was at least a minor brawl and a few broken bones on the Board to settle even trivial matters. The civilized approach left him with an uneasy feeling.

"Dice it is," Ashmed announced. "For such a weighty decision, I will require a broader probability distribution."

From his pocket, he produced a second of the remarkable Nagas. Sealiah graciously let him borrow her die.

"Highest and lowest numbers shall have sanction to wage open war," Ashmed explained. "The victor shall have all the usual rights of spoils."

"Fine," Lev grumbled. "Just let me roll those bones."

Ashmed raised an eyebrow at his impudence. The Chairman rolled first, the dice tumbling onto the table. They came to rest neatly on the pass line. A five and a four—hands touching stars—nine total.

Lev scooped up the dice, scowled, shook them violently, and threw.

The dice cracked together like a billiard break—bounced against the far bumpers, and rolled back in front of him. Four and three—seven: dead center in the probability distribution. The worst possible roll.

Lev's giant hands clenched about the table's railing and crushed it. He swallowed his rage, muttering.

Infernals heeded no rules . . . save one: No one ever went back on an agreement once dice were on the table.

Abby set her pet locust down, and it skittered out under the door. She stood on her tiptoes to reach the dice and rolled next.

A pair of the dancing dogs. Four. The lowest result yet.

She turned to Sealiah, challenge glimmering in her red eyes.

Sealiah toyed with the dice on the table, as if she could commune with their delectable randomness. She snatched them up and, with one graceful toss, sent them flying across the table, bouncing off the far end— impacting each other and coming to rest in the center. Two sixes, twelve crows on the wing—a *murder*, so called, or more commonly among mortals, *boxcars*, as they resembled a pair of freight cars on a train.

"Congratulations," Ashmed said. "We have one side." He looked between Sealiah and Abby. "Perhaps a matchup?" The Chairman's face was unreadable.

"Perhaps . . ." Sealiah plucked up the dice. To Louis's astonishment, she offered them to him.

Louis held up both hands. "I'm no Board member. I have no place in this."

In truth, he had no place because he was not a tenth as powerful as his cousins. Engaging in a war with a landed Infernal Lord was guaranteed suicide.

"You were present when we voted," Ashmed said. "I do not remember specifically excluding you." He pointed his smoldering cigar at Louis. "Your children should care for you more than for any of us. So your involvement would guarantee them running to your aid."

Sealiah smiled. "The way I hear it, they might run to aid his destruction." Her hand remained outstretched, offering him the dice.

"Stop squirming," Lev told him. "Roll." He took a step closer, one meaty hand curling into a titanic fist.

"Well . . ." Louis's smile never wavered as he reached for the dice. "Since you insist. I am honored."

He grabbed the cubes without touching Sealiah.

Louis tilted his palm . . . and with the most undramatic of gestures let the dice fall.

The cubes bounced onto the table once and stopped: a one and a two. A total of three.

His heart skipped a beat.

Abby growled and stamped her foot.

"It seems, Louis, we are fated to dance once more," Sealiah said.

"Not so fast, peddler of poppies," Mephistopheles said.

Talons raked the Nagas of Dharma across the green felt. Mephistopheles grabbed them, shook, and tossed. They came to rest directly in front of Sealiah: a pair of the self-consuming ouroboros serpents.

She flinched. "Snake eyes," Sealiah said. "How appropriate."

Louis almost fell over with relief.

Mephistopheles vanished. Only shadows remained where he had once stood.

"So be it," Ashmed declared. "The Board sanctions Civil War between Sealiah, Queen of Poppies, and Mephistopheles, Lord of the House of Umbra." He glanced at Louis with disdain. "You are dismissed."

The door behind him squeaked open.

"Happy to have been of assistance." Louis bowed and scraped and stepped backward and bowed once more—as the door slammed shut in his face.

"Too close," he breathed.

Louis turned in time to see Amberflaxus tearing the head off Abigail's locust, munching and crunching its fat body.

"Come, my friend," Louis whispered. "There's much to prepare. Chaos and opportunity abound today!"

He paused, however, wondering if placing his children in the greatest of dangers had been the best possible outcome.

For him—yes.

But what of them?

There was a faint, annoying whisper of doubt, a remnant of his mortal being. . . . Perhaps in time, it would go away like a blister healed after being popped.

No matter. He had plans and schemes and double-crosses to orchestrate.

5

PLACEMENT AND DISPLACEMENT

The Clock Tower chimed its ninth bell as Fiona and Eliot trampled up the worn marble steps of Bristlecone Hall.

There was a central yard dominated by a large silver tree, and classrooms extended to either side. Four doors down on the right was a sign: PLACEMENT EXAMS.

They sprinted for it, crossing the threshold of the classroom as the tenth and last bell sounded.

Panting, ready to fall over, Fiona saw one wall was floor-to-ceiling panes of glass—panes as small as a postage stamp on up to bedsheet-sized, and each slightly tilted or out of focus, magnifying or inverting the image of the old tree in the yard.

Her eyes adjusted to the darker room and she saw twelve rows of desks, twelve deep. They had rolled tops, ancient inkwells, attached stools that swung out, and wrought-iron footrests. At the front of this room was a massive blackboard, and along the walls were gaslight globes of opal glass.

As the last bit of her vision cleared, Fiona saw students at all the desks save two—and *all the students* turned to stare at Eliot and her.

"S-s-sorry," she said, and flushed.

"Apologize only if there is reason to," said a woman with a slight British accent.

This woman was the only person standing in the classroom besides Fiona and Eliot. She might have been thirty years old, and wore a long black skirt and a high-necked linen shirt with black pearl buttons. Her dark hair was up, and she wore octagonal spectacles that magnified her eyes.

She wasn't human.

The woman's skin and features were too perfect, too pale, more alabaster than organic, like a Greek statue.

Or perhaps an Immortal.

There was something else, too, in her brown-eyed stare. Fiona felt herself fall into that gaze until the world was swallowed. Fiona had felt this before, staring down the endless maw of Sobek, the crocodile eater of souls.

It was death. It was oblivion.

Fiona blinked, came out of the trance, and shuddered.

The woman opened a tiny leather book and consulted it. "Miss Fiona and Master Eliot Post." She made marks with a fountain pen. "On time." She spared them a glance. "By the skin of your teeth. Sit."

Fiona and Eliot obeyed, taking the only two unoccupied desks halfway to the front, on opposite sides of the center aisle.

The woman walked to the lectern. "I am Miss Westin, the Headmistress of the Paxington Institute," she said. "I wield absolute authority here."

No one spoke or shifted in their seats.

"You will find today's placement exam in your desks," Miss Westin continued, "along with three pencils and an eraser. See that you have these materials now. Do *not* break the seal on the examination."

Every student opened a rolltop desk.

In hers, Fiona found a stack of twenty pages secured with a cardboard band. All three pencils had been sharpened to a deadly point.

Miss Westin waited as the students settled down, keenly observing all. "I am delighted that you can follow instructions."

Fiona swallowed and heard the collective inhalation of the other students.

"You will find," Miss Westin said, "that at Paxington, we take our rules seriously. Last year, two students prematurely opened their examinations and were expelled."

Fiona felt like she was going to faint or throw up. Had Miss Westin briefed everyone on other rules before she and Eliot got here? What if they made a mistake?

She caught a motion in the corner of her eye.

The boy on her left waved to her. He was cute, with brown curly hair to his shoulders, and expressive eyes. He flashed a smile, nodded reassuringly, and then turned his attention back to Miss Westin.

Those simple gestures eased her fear. Fiona wanted to thank the boy, but thought better of doing so while Miss Westin spoke.

Miss Westin produced a silver pocket watch and flipped it open. "We shall begin the examination in sixty-four seconds. You will have one hour twenty minutes—which is four minutes per page—to finish. Budget your time accordingly."

One boy near the windows raised his hand. "If I break one of these marvelous writing implements?" he asked, brandishing a pencil.

Fiona recognized the Scottish accent. She squinted against the glare. Yes . . . it took a second for her to be sure . . . the blond hair, the roguish grin: it *was* Jeremy Covington, the boy she and Robert had found in the Valley of the New Year. He had escaped with them.

But the Valley was part of Purgatory. That meant Jeremy had been dead, didn't it?

"You have two spares, Mr. Covington," Miss Westin told him. "I suggest you break no more than three."

"And if I need the little boys' room, ma'am?" There was an undertone of smarm to his question.

Miss Westin stared him down. "Then I shall escort you myself to the urinal."

Jeremy's head dropped, and Fiona saw his ears redden.

"Hey," Eliot whispered. "Good luck!"

You, too, she mouthed back.

Four other older students entered the room.

Miss Westin nodded to them as they took positions in the corners. Miss Westin then glanced at her watch. "Begin . . . *now.*"

A hundred-some cardboard bands ripped, and a multitude of pages turned, sounding like a flock of birds taking wing.

The first section was on history. That should be a breeze. Fiona and Eliot had studied all of history from Earth's formation to global warming.

There were questions on Egyptian pharaohs, the reasons for the American Civil War, and influences on the Industrial Revolution.

She answered them all—could have done it in her sleep.

She turned to the next page, and there was a list of events to be chronologically ordered: Sargon and the formation of the Akkadian Empire . . . the discovery of the Americas . . . the founding of Rome by Romulus and Remus . . .

But Fiona froze when she got to, *King Arthur dies/ departs for Avalon.*

The tales of King Arthur had been banned by Audrey. *"Too many fairy tales and lies,"* she had told them.

Fiona scrunched her lips in irritation. She marked this with a question mark and moved on. She'd have to come back later and figure it out.

The next section was on mathematics.

She blasted through geometry and algebra problems, and slowed only a little on the trigonometry.

Fiona thought this was going well, but she wished she had a watch.

She looked around but spotted no clock. She did see, however, that Miss Westin walked the aisles, and the four older student proctors watched everyone with hawklike intensity.

Fiona noticed that Eliot (now wearing his spectacles) was ahead on his test, scribbling away on some essay.

She was about to get back to her test when she saw a girl three rows over staring at her. The girl had acne and long brown hair that fell into her face. Fiona knew her . . . but couldn't quite recall from where or when.

She turned back to her test; Fiona didn't want anyone to think she was cheating.

She focused on the next section: English.

Fiona knew all the great authors, their themes, styles, and techniques. In her comparative essay, she quoted Shakespeare and Shelley and Shaw from memory. She paused to admire her dramatic cursive handwriting before she flipped to the next section.

All her confidence drained as she read the heading: *Magic—Theory, Engineering, and History.*

Magic, legends, fairy tales, fantasy, and science fiction—all the things specifically forbidden in their household for the last fifteen years.

She took a deep breath, willed herself to stay calm.

The first question was, *Name the four classical elements, and discuss Plato's and Aristotle's inclusion of the fifth element.*

Five elements? There were more than *one hundred* elements: hydrogen, helium, carbon, nitrogen . . . Were they talking about something else?

She wouldn't panic. Not yet.

She skipped ahead to see if there were easier ones.

The next question was, *Name seven mortal magical families. Compare and contrast. Bonus: Name three extinct families.*

Mortal magical families? She knew there were Immortals, fallen angels . . . but there were *more* collections of magical people?

The back of Fiona's throat burned. She paged ahead.

There were questions on alchemy, divination, and necromancy.

How was she ever going to figure any of this out?

Next to her she heard pages rustle. She saw Eliot flip back and forth through this section as well —but then he stopped, and started scribbling.

He was guessing. Had to be.

It was just like Eliot to try something reckless when he didn't know the answer.

But why not? Miss Westin hadn't said it was forbidden.

Fiona set the tip of her pencil on the page, but couldn't force herself to write. It felt like a lie.

Across the classroom, she heard whispers. She ignored these voices and flipped back to the history section and King Arthur. If she had to make a guess, she'd make an *educated* one.

The whispers, however, got louder. There was a tiny laugh.

She looked up and saw Jeremy Covington, eyes sparkling, talking to a redheaded girl next to him—both had their test booklets closed, pencils set neatly on top. They were done already!

Jeremy had been just as rude in Purgatory: trying to kiss Fiona when he hadn't been invited to. She had a feeling he was going to be three times the trouble alive that he had been dead.

She couldn't waste energy thinking about him. She had to—

"Time!" Miss Westin announced, and snapped her pocket watch shut. "Pencils up."

Every student instantly complied.

Fiona was furious. She'd never *not* finished a test before.

She looked over to Eliot. He gave a little apologetic shrug, as if to say, *What can you do?*

There had to be something. She could claim extenuating circumstances—explain to Miss Westin about their weird mother and how they were brought up.

Miss Westin and the proctors moved to the head of each row. They picked up the test and graded them right in front of everyone—marking wrong answers with a red pen.

Miss Westin finished grading first and scrawled a large *D* on the front.

"Insufficient," Miss Westin told the crestfallen boy.

"We allow only those with the potential for excellence into Paxington, young man. You may leave."

The boy hung his head and skulked from the room.

This was so cruel. A trickle of molten iron anger flared within Fiona. She gripped the edge of her desk. Her nails dug into the wood, splitting the grain.

Ever since Fiona severed her appetite, she'd been unable to easily feel anything—except this sudden anger.

She imagined grabbing the desk and throwing it across the classroom and through the window. Destroying everything.

The shadow of Miss Westin crossed her gaze. "Test, Miss Post?"

Fiona's anger instantly quenched, as if it'd been plunged into liquid nitrogen. Chill bumps crawled over her arms.

"Yes, ma'am." She handed her the pages and noticed the Headmistress's hands were slender and bony.

Miss Westin flipped through the pages, barely making a mark until she got to the section on magic—and then she made a flurry of Xs.

It felt like the blood was draining out of her. Fiona wondered if she'd have the courage to stand and walk out of the classroom if she failed. What would she tell Audrey? Or the League?

Miss Westin turned to the cover, scribbled on it, and handed it back.

A fat red C stared at Fiona . . . which looked like it was laughing at her.

"Welcome to Paxington," Miss Westin said, and moved on.

Fiona stared at the grade. A C was barely passing, and failure by Audrey's standards. On the other hand— she exhaled—it was apparently sufficient to get her into Paxington.

She turned to Eliot for reassurance, but Miss Westin was grading his test, too.

She finished, leaving Eliot looking confused and worried . . . but also relieved. On the cover of his examination was a C+.

Fiona flashed him her test. "How did you do better?" she asked.

She *was* happy that he'd passed—Fiona couldn't even imagine what it would have been like if only one of them had gotten into Paxington—but how had he scored better?

Fiona watched as a girl behind her failed the test, and then two more students, who quickly picked up their bags and shuffled out of the room. Miss Westin was ruthless in her pronouncements to them: "failed . . . ," "insufficient . . . ," and ". . . you must now leave."

By the time she and the student proctors finished, one in ten had been dismissed.

Some students murmured: "*I heard one girl killed herself last year after she flunked out . . . ,*" and "*it's supposed to get* really *hard now,*" and "*fewer losers around here—good.*"

That last cruel remark had come from the redheaded girl next to Jeremy. She looked inordinately pleased with her test, which she held up so everyone could see her A–.

Miss Westin returned to the lectern.

Everyone fell silent.

"Welcome, freshman class, to the Paxington Institute," Miss Westin told them. Sunlight reflected off her glasses and made her eyes appear luminous and preternaturally large. "We will now cover some basics."

She pushed on the blackboard, revealing another blackboard behind it covered with pie charts and handwriting so perfect it made Fiona's look like epileptic scratches. Miss Westin indicated the title: *Mandatory Courses for First-Semester Freshmen.*

"All freshmen have two classes their first semester," she explained. "Mythology 101, in which I shall be your instructor, and gym class, taught by Mr. Ma."

Mythology? Was that the equivalent of their family history? She and Eliot might actually learn something practical about their world.

But gym class? Calisthenics, running, and softball? The thought of wearing skimpy shorts and a T-shirt and competing with other girls gave Fiona pause. And what about Eliot?

She glanced at him. His glasses had come off, and he looked more pale than normal. He hated sports. He'd always been smaller than boys his age. Cee said he would grow quick once puberty hit, and one day be tall and strong.

Fiona doubted that. Eliot would always be her "little brother," no matter what.

The redhead next to Jeremy Covington raised her hand. "Ma'am?" She had a Scottish accent as well, but far more refined. "What about electives? Will two courses be enough?"

Miss Westin fixed her with a stare. "These two classes, I assure you, will be sufficient. One quarter of the freshman class fail and do not continue on to their sophomore year."

The Headmistress pointed to a pie chart and a bell-shaped curve on the blackboard. "Success is based on a strict academic curve and your ranked performance in gym class." She crossed her hands. "At Paxington, only excellence is allowed."

That seemed grossly unfair. If one quarter failed *every* year—Fiona did the math—then only 42 percent made it through to their senior year.

But maybe competition wouldn't be such a bad thing. It would give her a chance to test herself, and prove that she could succeed outside Audrey's protected sphere.

"If you feel the need to be further challenged," Miss Westin continued, "elective courses are available for freshmen who survive their first semester and receive As on their midterms."

Survive?

Fiona and Eliot shared a look. Her word choice seemed deliberate . . . like some students might actually die.

Eliot definitely appeared unhealthy as he digested this statement. Fiona suddenly didn't feel so good, either.

"You will now have a break to stretch and use the restrooms before the next portion of the placement process," Miss Paxton said. "Afterward, you will be given a tour of the campus."

Fiona exhaled and heard the rest of the students do the same.

"This is so weird," Eliot said. He stood and stretched. "I feel like I don't belong here . . . but at the same time, I don't know, it's like we do."

She knew exactly what he meant. Part of her just wanted to go back home and hide. Another part of her wanted to meet some of these people from other magical families. Well . . . except that Jeremy Covington.

The other students mingled and talked, moving through the room like free-floating planets in orbit about one another, and then clustered around maybe a half-dozen individuals who appeared to be the centers of social gravity.

Fiona spotted the boy who had smiled at her and

made her feel welcome . . . but he was across the room now, chatting with some other boys and laughing.

Fiona and Eliot stood by themselves.

Would they always be social outcasts? If only the others knew they were in the League of Immortals—that Eliot was an Immortal hero, and she was a goddess-in-training.

But, of course, telling anyone the most interesting thing about themselves was forbidden. So typical.

"We should strike up a conversation," she told her brother.

"What do you want to talk about?" he asked.

"I mean with the others."

"Oh . . . ," Eliot said, looking a tad hurt. "Yeah, sure." He brightened. "You know, I thought I saw someone I recognized." He looked around.

"So did I," Fiona said. "That girl with the brown hair."

Eliot squinted. "No . . . I saw this other girl, a blonde, kind of looked like Julie."

"Julie Marks?" Fiona said, surprised.

Poor Eliot. Daydreaming again.

Fiona then spotted a group marching toward them, and leading them was that redhead and Jeremy Covington.

The last time Fiona had seen Jeremy, he wore a lion mask—which was then knocked off when Robert Farmington plastered him with a snowball. That was in Purgatory, at a cursed never-ending party called the Valley of the New Year.

Jeremy stopped before her and Eliot, and bowed so his long blond hair cascaded off his shoulders.

"Dearest Fiona," he said. "Never in a million years did I expect to see you again. I so wanted to thank you for saving me from my long imprisonment."

Eliot nudged her and shot her a look that said, *Who is this?*

"Jeremy, this is my brother, Eliot."

Eliot offered his hand for Jeremy to shake.

Jeremy clasped it and squeezed. Eliot winced.

"Damn my manners," Jeremy said. "I am Lord Jeremy of the Clan Covington." He gestured to the redheaded girl next to him. "This lass is my cousin Sarah." He spared a glance at the students around him, as though considering whether to introduce them as well, but then shrugged as if they were inconsequential.

Sarah's long hair, elegantly tied up, was the color of tangerines. She had dimpled cheeks, freckled skin, and Fiona could see the effect she had on the boys.

"Post . . . ," Sarah said. "I'm not familiar with your family's name. Were you sponsored into Paxington?"

This sounded like an innocent question on the surface, but Fiona sensed a hint of condescension underneath.

"No one sponsored us," Fiona said. She changed subjects to avoid the League and its code of silence. "I don't understand something," she said to Jeremy. "You were in Purgatory. There are only supposed to be dead people there. How can you be here . . . alive?"

Jeremy laughed. "No, my dear Fiona. Not dead. Never dead. It would take more than a trifling thing like Purgatory to stop a Covington."

6

§

NOT A POPULARITY CONTEST

Eliot took a step back from Jeremy and Sarah Covington. They were smiling, but he got the feeling it wasn't because they liked him. More like they were making a joke.

Fiona was no help. She wasn't paying attention to them; instead, she scanned the other students.

"You see," Jeremy said, continuing with his story, "the year was 1853, and I was chasing a leprechaun."

"What's a leprechaun?" Eliot asked.

Jeremy's and Sarah's smiles faltered, and the students around them gave Eliot a weird look, like he'd just asked what oxygen was.

Then Jeremy grinned again. "So true! Who really knows what they be, eh? Pots of gold and three wishes—balderdash, I entirely agree. That's what I set out to prove: The Fey be not the living legends all claim."

Eliot nodded, realizing this was something he ought to have known.

"So the thing led me on a merry chase through every swamp and graveyard in Scotland," Jeremy said. "Thought she could lose me with a romp through the Middle Realms, but I followed her right to the bloody center of Purgatory . . . where I got a bit distracted."

Middle Realms. Eliot made a mental note about

that, but didn't ask any more questions. No need to look like a complete idiot.[6]

"You got trapped in the Valley of the New Year," Fiona said, her attention returning to the conversation.

"Why, yes, dearest Fiona," Jeremy replied. "Then you came along and found the doorway out of that wretched place. Rescued me, body and soul."

Sarah's heart-shaped face brightened, and she reassessed Fiona. "So this is the girl who brought you back? The Clan Covington is in your debt, miss."

Fiona fiddled with her hair. "It was nothing, really."

"Wait . . . ," Eliot said. "You were trapped for over a hundred and fifty years?"

"Aye." Jeremy shrugged. "You might say I'm starting my freshman year at Paxington a tad delayed."

The Headmistress returned. A dozen older students entered with her, and some moved to the windows, drawing long black curtains, while others turned up the gas lamps on the opposite wall.

Miss Westin removed her glasses. She looked different in gaslight: younger, more animated, and vital. A faint smile crossed her pale lips.

"Team selection is starting," Sarah said, and touched Jeremy's arm.

"Aye." Jeremy tensed and cast a quick glance at Fiona and Eliot.

Eliot didn't like the sound of this "team" stuff. He wasn't good in groups.

---

6. Middle Realms (noun). Archaic usage refers to the Purgatory lands betwixt Heaven and Hell (sometimes Earth, depending on the context). Modern usage expanded to mean *all* realms between the Pearly Gates of Heaven and the First Fathomless Abyss of Hell (considered the upper and lower boundaries of the known worlds). *Lexicon Primus*. Paxington Institute Press LLC, San Francisco.

Miss Westin cleared her throat, and everyone in the room was quiet. "Freshman team selection," she said, "is a tradition that dates to the foundation of this school.[7]

"It tests your skills of diplomacy and strategic thinking. I advise you to combine disparate elements to make something greater than the sum of its parts." Every trace of warmth and color drained from Miss Westin's expression. "This should *not* be a popularity contest."

She motioned to the side door, and more upperclassmen entered, carrying claw-footed tables. They set them at the head of the room. On each table were silver trays containing gold coins.

Miss Westin gestured to each tray and said, "Knight . . . Wolf . . . Dragon . . . Hand . . . Eagle . . . and Scarab—in their various incarnations. These will be the symbols about which you must unite with seven other students."

Eliot glanced at the Paxington crest on his jacket. Those same symbols hovered over his heart, part of the school's history.

He looked at Fiona. She shrugged, looking as awkward and uncomfortable as he felt—like they were two guppies in a tank of piranhas.

Jeremy swaggered up to a table. "I, Jeremy Covington, of the Clan Covington, Keeper of the Keys of the

---

7. Freshman team selection at Paxington originates from the gladiatorial arenas of the Roman Empire. Slaves who won their freedom could leave or continue as paid gladiators. Such free fighters would often participate in re-creations of famous battles, but unlike slave gladiators, they were allowed to form their own teams. The victorious teams were glorified throughout the Empire (much like modern-day sports teams), bearing names like Hunting Wolf, Golden Eagle, and the Bloodied Hand. *Your Guide to the Paxington Institute (Freshman Edition).* Paxington Institute Press LLC, San Francisco.'

Three Stones, hereby claim Scarab as mine." He plucked up one of the coins and showed it to everyone. Upon it gleamed a golden scarab like something lifted off an Egyptian pharaoh's tomb.

Eliot whispered to Fiona, "Are we supposed to go up there and take one of those things?"

Before she could answer, a tall pale boy strode to a different table. "I, Donald of the Family Van Wyck, claim Wolf as my standard."

Sarah Covington moved to Jeremy's side and proudly took a scarab token.

And then another two girls and three more boys moved forward to various tables.

"Logan from the Kaleb brood takes Green Dragon."

"I, Xavier of the DeBoars, claim the Open Hand."

"The Family Pern is Soaring Eagle and challenges all who say otherwise!"

The room erupted into chaos as almost every other student moved for the tables—talking and arguing and snatching up tokens.

Eliot spied that blond girl he had seen before. There was just a flash of her face, and she vanished into the crowds. She *did* look a little like Julie Marks, the girl he had fallen for this summer. Julie was long gone, but he never stopped thinking about her.

Then he spotted another girl with long uncombed brown hair. She looked familiar, too. Maybe that was the girl Fiona had mentioned.

The girl caught Eliot's gaze and quickly looked away.

"Eliot!" some boy called out.

Eliot spun about, trying to locate the voice, but with all the students pushing and embroiled in heated discussions, Eliot couldn't find him.

He was disoriented and completely out of his depth.

"This is some sort of test, too," he said to Fiona. "Part of the placement exam."

"I get that," Fiona replied. She wasn't looking at him.

Eliot followed her gaze and spotted a boy who approached Jeremy and Sarah. He had a tousle of curly brown hair, an easy smile, and looked totally relaxed here. He bowed to Sarah and struck up a conversation with the Covingtons.

"Let's see how it's done," Eliot suggested.

But Fiona had already started to move toward them.

The boy told Jeremy, "I was unaware the Covington clan claimed Scarab."

"Goes all the way back to the Freemasons," Jeremy explained, his voice a mixture of insult and amazement that someone would question his claim. He looked the other boy over. "Be that the challenge, Mr.—?"

The other boy spotted Eliot and Fiona as they approached, and his smile warmed. "No challenge," he said. "I'm Mitch from the Stephenson family. I wanted to join."

"Stephenson?" Jeremy's eyes widened a fraction. "Indeed! A family with as noble a pedigree as the Covingtons. It would be an honor, sir." He shook Mitch's hand.

"As noble as they are clever and handsome," Sarah added.

"My cousin Sarah," Jeremy said.

Sarah offered her hand to Mitch, which he clasped. Eliot noted slight disappointment on Sarah's face, as if she had wanted him to kiss it or something.

Fiona pulled Eliot closer and said, "We should join Scarab."

"You told me this Jeremy guy was kind of creepy. I'm not sure he or his cousin likes us."

Eliot glanced around the room. No other team had three people on it yet, and a few of the discussions had evolved into shouting matches.

"But they do seem to know the ropes around here," Fiona said.

Three other freshmen approached Jeremy and Sarah. They spoke briefly, but Jeremy held up both his hands and shook his head. The other students left, muttering a few words that Eliot (even with his extensive vocabulary) had never heard before.

"Definitely Anglo-Saxon etymology," Fiona told him, apparently also curious about these new words. She nudged Eliot. "We should ask them now. I don't want to be the last ones picked."

Eliot reluctantly stepped forward. She was right: Anything was better than getting picked last. Or worse, what if all the other groups became so full that he and Fiona had to go on *different* teams?

"Ah, Fiona." Jeremy extended a hand to her as she neared. "Please join us"—a quick glance at Eliot— "and, of course, your brother."

His gaze, however, slid over Eliot like he was something one saw on a dinner plate, unpalatable, but which had to be tasted in order to get dessert.

Sarah eyed Eliot as well, leaned closer to Jeremy, and said something.

"Yes," Jeremy told her. "I'm quite sure."

Eliot loathed this. Was he getting on the team only because Jeremy liked his sister?

He should've been picked because he was Eliot Post, Immortal hero-in-training, Master of "The Symphony of Existence," son of the Eldest Fate and the Prince of Darkness!

If only he could tell them . . . he would've been their *first* choice.

He could turn them down, too. He would have challenged one of those supposedly blue-blooded mortal magicians, taken one of their big-deal tokens, and started his own team.

But this daydream faded as the girl Eliot had seen before caught his attention.

She walked straight toward him. Her long hair fell into her face, and her gaze firmly fixed upon the floor . . . reminding him of the way Fiona used to be so shy. Yet, without looking, she somehow managed to navigate through the crowds, halting before Eliot. "Hey . . . ," she said. "I never got the chance to thank you or your sister." She looked up, and the hair fell from her face.

The girl was unremarkable save for her eyes. They were dark, wild, and defiant—like black coals, smoldering. The last time Eliot saw them, the world had been on fire, and they were running for their lives through a burning carnival, being chased by madman Perry Millhouse.

"Amanda?" he said. "It's Amanda Lane, right?"

"Yeah." Amanda looked back to the floor.

"Are you okay?" Fiona asked. "We never got a chance to see you after . . ."

"Sure, I'm great," she said, although the way she struggled to get her words out, Eliot guessed otherwise. "Your uncle got me back to my family. He was great. He talked to them. Explained how I got kidnapped. How you guys saved me. I dunno, my parents never mentioned it after that."

Eliot wondered what Uncle Henry had done. He had an uneasy feeling something more was going on with Amanda Lane and the League.

"Then I got the scholarship," Amanda said, "everything paid by Mr. Mimes. He said I belonged here." She looked around. "I'm not so sure this was a good idea."

Something was weird about this. Why would Uncle Henry bring a normal girl here after she'd almost been killed once by the League?

Eliot glanced at Fiona, and she nodded back, thinking the same thing.

"Stick close to us," Fiona whispered to Amanda.

Eliot was going to add his own words of reassurance, but all thoughts drained from his head when he spotted the blond girl who had caught his attention before . . . as she moved toward them.

She most definitely was not Julie Marks, however. This girl was taller. Her hair was pure platinum blond that curled into ringlets about her face. Her skirt seemed shorter than the other girls'. She moved with a liquid grace that made Eliot's heart beat faster.

In fact, every boy watched her as she stopped before their table.

"M'lady," Jeremy said, and bowed ridiculously low before her. Mitch gave her a cordial bow, which provoked a raised eyebrow from this new girl. Sarah and Fiona simultaneously crossed their arms.

"Would you do us the honor of joining our team?" Jeremy asked. "We have two from glorious Clan Covington, a lad from the most ancient Stephenson family, Fiona and Eliot Post . . ." Jeremy searched for some embellishment or title to add to their family name, but failed.

The girl smiled. It was Julie's hundred-watt smile, and yet so unlike Julie's, because while this one was just as dazzling, it was also somehow cruel.

"Your solicitation is as empty as your head," she told Jeremy. "You know not whom you ask, your eyes too full with too obvious intentions."

This insult seemed to please Sarah.

Jeremy opened his mouth to defend himself, but the blond girl ran right over him with her words: "I am Jezebel, Protector of the Burning Orchards and Duchess of the Many-Colored Jungle of the Infernal Poppy Kingdoms, Handmaiden to the Mistress of Pain . . . and bringer of doom to mortals such as you." Her smile never faltered. "*Now* ask me to join, if you dare."

The room went silent, and everyone watched.

She was an Infernal? Like Beelzebub? Or their father?.

Was that why Eliot felt that he knew her? He should be wary, but he was also fascinated.

"Aye," Jeremy said. His eyes could not meet hers. "There's been no Infernal protégée at Paxington for three hundred years. Your terrible power would honor us, Lady Jezebel."

Jezebel huffed a laugh. "You *are* a rogue, Covington. I appreciate that." She looked over Sarah, moving on quickly, as if the girl were nonexistent. Next she considered Mitch, who had the strength to meet her gaze, and she nodded. She then glanced at Eliot and Fiona—just for an instant, but clearly seeing something in them that she liked, because her eyes widened with interest. Her gaze traversed to Amanda, scrutinizing the unremarkable girl the longest.

"You have an interesting mix of blood and power on this team," Jezebel told Jeremy. "I suppose it will do as much as any other collection of bumbling mortals here."

Jeremy beamed, extremely pleased with this new addition to their group. He shot a glance at Amanda, probably wondering if Jezebel assumed she was on their team . . . and if he had to accept this new unexpected teammate because the Infernal obviously liked her. He sighed and with great reluctance slipped Amanda a scarab token and then looked away.

Jezebel moved to the edge of the table and, with a dramatic flounce, sat on it, crossing her legs so her skirt flashed pale, slender thigh.

A full-blooded Infernal on their team. Eliot could only imagine what kinds of advantages and disadvantages that would give them. On the other hand, he wasn't sure what kind of game they would be playing that they'd *need* an Infernal.

Weren't Infernals supposed to be unpredictable? Cheaters? Dangerous?

Students clambered about their table—all now asking to join. The sheer mass of the crowd pushed Eliot, Amanda, and Fiona back. Apparently, the Paxington students appreciated the power of an Infernal more than they feared one.

"Let chance decide," Jezebel said. She reached for the platter on the table, selected the last golden scarab token from the pile—and flung it across the room.

Before Jeremy could protest, students scrabbled and pushed to get the token as it clattered across the floor.

Jezebel laughed as she watched boys and girls wrestle for the coin.

Eliot watched, too, and saw someone he recognized tossing aside students like he was an experienced wrestler. But the gold coin rolled away from him—kicked back and forth by the others.

This had to be the person who had called to Eliot earlier.

. . . and if he were on Team Scarab, Eliot knew he'd have at least one friend.

Let *only* chance decide? Eliot would see about *that*.

He twisted around, unzipped his backpack, and opened his violin case.

With one eye, he watched the scarab coin wobble along the floor, spinning, then kicked up, bouncing over the desks.

Eliot quietly plucked Lady Dawn's strings.

The heat from his old infection burned along his wrist. He felt air move about him, and saw the coin jump to his notes—ricocheting this way and that—half random, but partially under his command now as well.

It drunkenly rolled toward the boy he knew—who dived for it!

Others leaped for the coin, too, dog-piling into a heap.

Eliot held his breath, hoping.

He quickly surveyed his team: Fiona, his ever-irritating sister; Amanda Lane, more of a social outcast than even himself; Jeremy and Sarah Covington, whom Eliot didn't like one bit; Mitch Stephenson, a nice guy; and the Infernal Jezebel, who stared at Eliot and his backpack, leaning forward, one hand over her throat, fascinated.

. . . and one last teammate.

The boy stood up from the pile of students, holding aloft the golden scarab.

He turned and faced them, grinning, blood on his split lip. His James Dean appearance looked out of place in a Paxington jacket instead of his normal leather one.

Fiona gasped.

It was Robert Farmington.

7

THE FOOL'S OPENING MOVE

Henry Mimes changed names like other men changed their hats. Along with his nom de guerre shifts, he altered his personality, often becoming the Name.

Earlier this morning, he had been the Messenger. Now, though, as he stood close to Audrey in the private elevator that whisked them to the top of the Transamerica Building, he felt an impulse to try on the Big Bad Wolf.

Audrey wore a dark silk blouse and looked as she had in the old days, clad in similar cold colors, offsetting her alabaster skin. The Pale Rider. She and her sisters were the first of them to show greatness; she was the first woman he had ever called a "goddess."

She ignored him.

Lovely? Yes. Even more important: unattainable. Audrey was as perfect as a woman could be.

Her diamond earrings cast a scattering of reflections over her shoulders and throat . . . her skin was so lustrous. One touch and he knew he could warm that stone-cold flesh. How lonely she must be.

His hand rose toward her.

But he sensed the lines of deadly force radiating from her.

Henry reconsidered and dropped his hand. Perhaps the Fool best suited today's dismal occasion.

"Did you know," Henry asked her, "that San Franciscans call the Transamerica Building—?"

"Pyramid," Audrey corrected him. "It is the Transamerica *Pyramid*."

"Quite right. They also call it the Great Alien Ring Toss. Others say it looks like an ice cream cone stuck into the earth."

Audrey turned, raised an eyebrow, but said nothing.

So much for his attempt to lighten the Lady's mood.

Henry dug into his pocket and retrieved his silver hip flask, unstoppered it, paused to savor the scent of a thousand flowers, and then took a nip. The liquor exploded through his thoughts, leaving curlicues of smoke and memory. He exhaled the vapors.

In truth, Henry's mood needed lightening as much as Audrey's did. He was attempting to think six moves ahead of the Council *and* the Infernal Board—a worthy challenge for any fool.

Or perhaps he was taking this affair with the twins too seriously?

He took another drink and offered the flask to Audrey. This was just for politeness's sake. Never in a million years would Audrey join him. The sun and moon were more likely to unexpectedly eclipse.

Audrey mashed the EMERGENCY STOP button and took the flask.

How wonderful! Someone other than himself had done something surprising.

Audrey inhaled the bouquet, and her pupils dilated. "It would be less dangerous to carry refined plutonium through the city than real Soma." She took a long pull, to Henry's dismay, drinking nearly half. A rare blush spread outward from her neck.

She handed the flask back and said, "I assume you

have countless layers of trickery planned with regard to my children?"

Henry put on his best *How could you ever think such a thing? You wound me, woman* look, and then stammered, "If only you knew how much I care for Eliot and Fiona."

"I know," she said, "but sometimes, Henry, people would be better off without any of us 'caring' about them."

She set a hand on his chest—the lightest of touches.

Henry wasn't sure where this was going, for Audrey never casually touched anything. He backed into a corner of the elevator.

Audrey pressed closer and remained with him. Her fingers dug into his black turtleneck. "I sense your heart beating and feeling. You do care for them . . . as much as any of us can."

She grasped a handful of his shirt.

The threads in the weave constricted about Henry's ribs.

"As long as by 'caring for Eliot and Fiona' you mean you have *their* best interests in mind—and not *yours*."

Henry started to protest, but found the air gone from his lungs.

"Did you know Fiona has learned the trick of cutting with string?" Audrey asked. "She has yet to discover that it can also be done with *many* strings at once . . . like woven cloth."

Audrey pulled his shirt taut.

Henry had a sudden vision of Audrey ripping the shirt from his torso—like some stage magician trick—only this would not be trickery . . . and what would remain of his torso would fit through a martini strainer.

Audrey let go.

She tapped the EMERGENCY STOP button. The elevator continued up.

Henry recovered and straightened his turtleneck. He took one more swig from his flask.

The elevator doors parted, and cold fresh air blasted them.

They stepped onto the uppermost secret level of the Transamerica Pyramid.

The aluminum shutters on the angled walls were open, and mid-morning light streamed into the space. This level of the pointy part of the landmark building had been filled with dust bunnies before he'd had it renovated. The space had been redecorated with ultramodern velvet couches (designed in the 1960s, when there actually had been a vision of an ultramodern future).

Of course, the family was already here.

Lucia, Henry noticed first—Audrey's sister, the Middle Fate, and sometimes called (although he thought with the greatest irony), Blind Justice. Then there was Gilbert, known first as Gilgamesh, whom Henry fondly remembered as the Once-King. Kino was next, the Guardian of the Underworld, dour and sour and unsociable as ever. And last was old Cornelius, what was left of the last of the Titans, the once mighty Cronos.

Lucia sat opposite the elevator, a strategic location where she could chastise those who came late. She wore a gray power business suit with bloodred pinstripes. It was conservatively sexy. The steel in her gaze communicated to Henry that she would tolerate none of his usual tomfoolery today.

So he would have to invent all-new tomfoolery for the occasion.

Gilbert crossed the room, a bottle of tequila in one

hand, two glasses in the other. He poured Henry a tumbler, and one for himself. "Too auspicious a day to face sober, Cousin."

Henry nodded and took the glass. Gilbert looked disheveled, his golden beard wild and dark circles under his eyes.

But when Henry sipped the drink, he found it disappointingly only iced tea.

Gilbert maintained pretenses, still silently on Henry's side in this matter . . . part of their very, very long-range strategy. Henry was relieved to know that the First King Gilgamesh was still as smart as ever.

"Have you heard?" Gilbert gestured with his drink to a corner bathed in sunlight. "We have a *special* guest with us today."

Henry squinted. Camouflaged in the radiance was Dallas.

Poor Dallas had been kicked off the Council last week, replaced with her older sister, Audrey. Lucia had thought her too soft. That was a mistake, Henry feared, that Lucia would one day pay for dearly.

Dallas wore a sundress of translucent sea green, high-heeled sandals, and carried a Versace clutch. The breeze made her dress and golden hair ripple.

Henry took a step toward her, irresistibly drawn to Beauty . . . but then noted the look in her eyes was pure liquid-nitrogen venom. She was, of course, here under protest at the behest of a Council's summons. Henry understood it all in that instant—her part to play in their schemes and the intersibling politics—and checked his motion toward her.

The door to the emergency stairs banged open, and Aaron entered, lugging a duffel in one hand. He had marched up the forty-nine floors without breaking a sweat.

Aaron made a point of slamming the door. He dropped his duffel with a floor-shaking thud, shot everyone a glare, and then sat across from Lucia, propping his cowboy boots on the couch.

Tall, dark Kino spared him a deprecating glance. He then straightened the lily in the lapel of his black leather overcoat and turned to Audrey. "So good to see you, my dear. I think you shall be a voice of reason among this collection of fools."

"One hopes," Audrey replied as she settled next to Lucia.

"Shall we start?" Cornelius mumbled. "I believe everyone is finally present."

Cornelius was on the floor. He wore an I LOST MY HEART IN SF T-shirt, shorts, and athletic socks embroidered with tiny cable cars pulled up to his knobby knees. Good for him. Playing the tourist, preserving his childlike sense of discovery, was likely what kept the oldest living thing alive.

"Yes, all present," Lucia said, and smoothed back her hair, tying it up in a knot. She rang her tiny silver bell. "I hereby call the Council of Elders of the League of Immortals to order. *Narro, Audio, Perceptum.*"

Lucia set a hand delicately next to Audrey. "Can you give us an update on the twins? Are they well? How have they done at Paxington so far?" The illusion of her concern was nearly perfect.

"Of course," Audrey replied.

Henry drifted from the center of the room to the open shutters for fresh air.

"All has been arranged with Miss Westin," Audrey explained. "I've received word that Eliot and Fiona passed their entrance and placement exams."

"I dislike the twins at Paxington," Kino said, his lips compressing into a line.

"It is neutral ground," Lucia replied, "open only to students and staff. It is the safest place from the Infernals. Besides, Eliot and Fiona may learn a thing or two."

"It is Paxington's neutrality that concerns me," Kino told her. "Now is the time for *choosing* sides—the right side—*our* side! Paxington harbors those who would not join us, and over the centuries, they have grown strong within those walls. Why? To preserve the magical knowledge of the world? Are any of us that naïve? They await an opportune time to strike."

Cornelius cleared his throat. "It is a possibility," he said. "Their Headmistress, however, is the chief enforcer of the 1852 Treaty of the Under-Realms. She alone keeps the peace with the London Confederation of the Unliving. Move against her, and I fear that would be undone."

Kino shook his head. "Even more reason for the twins not to be there: Her kind should never be permitted near a child."

"Do not forget their Gatekeeper, Harlan Dells," Aaron told him. "Quite the feat, dismantling his own bridge as he left us. One does not lightly engage in combat with the One Who Can Be in Many Places . . . not unless you're proposing a full-scale war?"[8]

Lucia rolled her eyes. "The Council is *not* debating this. Paxington keeps the mortal magical families com-

---

8. The Bifröst Bridge connected Earth (Midgard) with the realm of the gods (Asgard). It was defended by the god Heimdallr (aka Heimdall, who will alert the Immortals to Ragnarök). Early myths depict the Bifröst Bridge as a shimmering rainbow that can appear and vanish. Modern interpretations suggest a dimensional shift. The theory lends credence to the rumor of the bridge being destroyed and the remnants used in the walls of the San Francisco Paxington Institute (which anecdotally seems to move in and out of phase with this world). *Gods of the First and Twenty-first Century, Volume 6, Modern Myths.* Zypheron Press Ltd., Eighth Edition.

placent. Destroy their precious school, and they might unite, however unlikely, and threaten our power base. No, we require stability at the moment. After we deal with the Infernal issue . . . then we shall revisit Paxington."

Kino sighed, but then nodded.

"What team are they on?" Henry asked, hoping to deflect the subject.

"Scarab," Audrey replied.

"Hmm." Aaron stroked his Genghis Khan mustache. "That's a Covington heritage title. Must be one of those slippery characters in the mix. Not a bad thing: they'll know how to handle the other students. I still dislike the whole point of their gym class, and that Mr. Ma."

"You must get over your competitive streak with that man," Henry told him.

"He and I have unsettled business," Aaron muttered.

"In any event," Audrey continued, "Miss Westin was recalcitrant to keep their identities hidden . . . but she eventually came around to the Council's point of view."

Henry saw in the distance, nestled next to Presidio Park, the Paxington campus: copper-capped spires, the Clock Tower, manicured lawns, and sparkling quad. A bank of fog rolled past, and the school was hidden again.

Kino was correct: Paxington had its drawbacks. But Audrey was also wise to place the children there. It served many purposes: training them in the realities of their world, keeping them on neutral ground, where they would have the best protection possible . . . as well as being advantageous to *Henry's* schemes.

Henry had also approached the "recalcitrant" Headmistress of Paxington, the lonely and terrible Miss Westin. He adjusted the collar of his turtleneck and shuddered as he considered the price he had paid to engage her services.

"I am worried," Lucia said, "over the lack of Infernal response to our declaration of the twins' indoctrination. There's typically *some* response from their Board—even if it is insulting negation."

"It is the silence of collusion," Kino said, and narrowed his eyes at Henry. "I have no doubt they are taking action against us."

Aaron sat up. "On this I agree. We should act."

"But what action can we take against the other family?" Cornelius asked. "Our own neutrality treaty blocks us."

"We must cement the children's loyalties to the League," Audrey told them. "They are still young and impressionable. You must act to mold them before they are shaped by others."

Kino steepled his hands as he considered this.

Henry saw an opportunity. "I suggest we show the twins how wonderful it can be to be in the League." In a grand gesture he raised his hands to the sky. "So far— and I'm sure, Audrey, you had the best of intentions— they have been saddled with nothing but rules and regulations."

Audrey turned to him, and her short silver hair flashed like a halo. The look in her eyes, however, was anything but angelic.

"I offer my humble services to take young Master Eliot under my wing," Henry continued. "Nothing overt, I assure you. Just the odd trip to the ice-cream parlor. Perhaps the occasional man-to-man chat so he has a proper role model."

They all gave Henry a look.

"Oh, very well," Henry said with a shrug. "I'm sure

there are others better suited to being a role model. My point is still valid."

"I agree," Lucia said. "We have already done some thinking along those lines. Henry is a suitable choice as emissary to young Eliot."

Henry wasn't sure where Lucia was going with this. Her agreeing with anything he said set off alarm bells.

"Additionally," Lucia continued, "Fiona will need someone to shepherd her, and convince her it is in her best interest to align with the League." She looked pointedly at Dallas. "Someone with a similar youthful exuberance . . ."

Dallas had been pretending to ignore her, looking at the vista of San Francisco, but she turned and said, "Is that why I was 'invited' to this meeting?" She scoffed. "Leave me out of your scheming, Sister. I'm not the Council's puppet. And I have no intention of candy-coating what it means to be Immortal—let alone a member of this League."

"Very well," Lucia replied. "No one is forcing you. We will find someone more willing." She tapped one manicured nail to her lower lip. "I wonder if Ish is available."

Dallas's eyes widened at this, and her hands curled into fists. "That Xanax-popping harlot? You can't be serious."

"We do need someone," Lucia told her. "And she is capable of having fun. . . ."

Dallas stifled a squeak of rage.

Outside the sun grew brighter, and the intense light made the metal walls ping as they heated and expanded.

Henry took a step away from both women.

It had been a mistake to collect all three Fates in

one location—explosive, primer, and detonator all in one neat package.

Dallas sighed, however, and hung her head. "Very well. I'll do it."

"Excellent," Lucia purred. "Do I have a second to the motion for Henry to mentor Eliot, and Dallas to bring along Fiona?"

"I will second," Gilbert said.

Lucia looked surprised that her recently estranged lover would so readily agree to her suggestion.

Henry worried that he had overplayed their hand. . . .

Lucia nonetheless continued: "Shall we put it to a vote?"

"Wait," Kino said, his dark, ever-skeptical eyes taking them all in. "Only with honey will you bribe the children? There is a more potent method to convince them our ways are best. With fear."

Aaron stood, color flushing his already ruddy cheeks.

Cornelius made little calming-down motions with his hands. "Let us hear what he has to say."

Aaron nodded and sank back down.

Kino smiled. "Show them the benefit of the League, yes, I agree. But also show them the opposite side of the coin: the *disadvantages* of the *other* family."

Audrey nodded, understanding. "You want to scare the hell out of them," she said. "Literally. Perhaps . . ." Her features hardened. "But *only* scare them, Kino."

The two stared at each other a moment, and then Kino blinked and gave a tiny bow. "Of course."

"And who better to do this," Lucia asked, "but the Lord of the Dead and Guardian of the Gateway to Hell?"

A chill spread down Henry's spine. Indeed, Lucia and Kino had schemes of their own hatching.

But there were worse alternatives to so influencing young Eliot and Fiona—ones no one here spoke of—yet. If the Infernals brought them over to their side . . . the League had signed Warrants of Death for both children.

The bright sunlight faded. Iron gray clouds covered the sky.

This was a possibility Henry would do anything to avoid, or at least delay its inevitability for as long as he could.

8

TOUR

Fiona waited outside in the courtyard. She welcomed the sunlight on her skin after being cooped up for so long. The classroom in Bristlecone Hall had felt like a tomb.

Without crossing into its shade, she examined the tree in the yard. It was a bristlecone pine with a silver trunk and skeletal arms that only occasionally sprouted a pine needle. This species could live for thousands of years, like her family.

Was she Immortal as well? Fiona couldn't even imagine what it would be like to be 16 years old, let alone 116 . . . or 1,600.

The other freshman teams stood together in loose cliques across the courtyard: Green Dragon, Black Wolf,

White Knight, Soaring Eagle, and others. They talked and stole glances at each other.

Sixteen teams. Eight students in each yielded a total of 128 in their freshman class . . . of which a quarter, thirty-two of them, would fail.

Fiona had a bad feeling about this. Why couldn't school just be about reading and learning? Why was it so cutthroat?

She eyed that Jezebel girl, an Infernal—and so did almost every boy. They clustered around her, all smiling and flirting and wanting to know her better.

She did look a *little* like Julie Marks, but this girl was taller and older. Maybe Julie had had an older sister who'd crawled out of Hell.

And why was she getting all the attention? Because she was pretty. Beyond pretty, really: Jezebel had a mystical look, like she had just stepped out of a masterwork oil painting, luminous and perfect.

Fiona smoothed her skirt and jacket, thankful for the school uniforms. If she'd had to wear Cee's homemade clothes, the social chasm between her and the rest of these girls would have been light-years wide.

That may have been the most unfair thing of all. Fiona was a *goddess,* for crying out loud, and yet somehow she still managed to look *less* than ordinary.

Eliot shuffled closer to her. "What kind of mascot is a scarab?" he asked.

She tore her gaze away from Jezebel. "The Egyptian pharaohs used scarabs as symbols of eternal life."[9]

---

9. Scarab beetles bury dung balls for later use, which is invaluable, as this removes pest habitat and returns nutrients to the soil. The scarab in hieroglyphics translates as "to come into being," convey-

Fiona was about to engage Eliot in debate over hieroglyphics (her knowledge was rudimentary, but Eliot's was nonexistent) when Robert Farmington emerged from the restrooms, cleaned up from the scuffle to get that last token.

She brightened as he walked toward her.

He looked like he owned the entire school. That was so Robert's style.

But he also looked out of place in a Paxington school uniform—like someone dressed for Halloween. She half expected to see his motorcycle parked in the corridors.

Fiona didn't have a clue what Robert was doing here, but she didn't care.

She moved to meet him, and started to reach out and hug him, but that felt wrong in front of all these people . . . and besides, Robert made no such move toward her, stopping a short distance away.

"You didn't call after our vacation," she whispered. "Was there trouble?"

Robert looked away. "Some," he said. "After I got kicked out of the League, I had to lie low for a while. Mr. Mimes says I can't go back to work for him . . . so he got me in here. Kind of a going-away present."

"You're on your own?"

"Yeah," Robert said. "I've always been on my own. It's no big deal."

---

ing ideas of transformation and resurrection in ancient Egyptian religion and art. Given that the freshman year of the Post twins is cited as their key transformative year, mythohistorians have debated the symbolism, and the coincidence, of their having the scarab as their team symbol. *Gods of the First and Twenty-first Century, Volume 11, The Post Family Mythology.* Zypheron Press Ltd., Eighth Edition.

Robert spotted Eliot and waved. His gaze then fell upon Jezebel and darkened.

Fiona felt something wrong—very wrong—between her and Robert. The week they'd spent on a tropical island this summer was a distant dream. She wanted to take his hand, give it a reassuring squeeze, but the air between them chilled . . . and something inside her protectively curled away from him.

An older boy strode her way. It was the student she and Eliot had met before—the one who *hadn't* helped them find Paxington. His chiseled Italian features broke into a smile as he saw her. "I'm glad you passed the entrance and placement exams," the boy said. "I had a feeling you and your brother would."

Then to the rest of the group, the older boy said in a commanding voice, "I will be your guide today, Team Scarab. I am Dante of the family Scalagari. Please follow me."

Dante turned and they fell in behind him: Jeremy and Sarah Covington introducing themselves to the Scalagari boy, Jezebel parting with her entourage, Mitch Stephenson, and Robert, herself, and Eliot . . . followed at last by Amanda Lane.

"Scalagari is an old family," Robert whispered to Fiona and Eliot. "They weave magic. Usually the best-dressed guys in the place."

"What about the Covington clan?" Eliot asked.

"They're conjurers," Robert said. "Nine times out of ten, troublemakers to boot. I wouldn't waste time worrying about them, though. You've got bigger problems on your team."

He had to mean Jezebel.

Fiona wanted to ask Robert what exactly a conjurer was, but Dante turned, walking backward, and said,

"Paxington was founded in 329 C.E. in Rome by Emperor Constantine. He wanted to study Jewish and Pagan influences on Christianity. Called *Curia Deus Pax*, or 'the Court of God's Peace,' many believed its true purpose was to secretly eradicate those influences."[10]

Sarah Covington lagged behind and turned to Robert (completely ignoring Fiona and Eliot). "I'm Sarah," she said, and smiled so her freckled cheeks dimpled. She held out her hand.

Robert took her hand, clasping in a way that was more than a handshake . . . and only a little less than an embrace.

"The pleasure is mine," he said.

Fiona felt her blood heat.

"A most impressive scuffle to get our token."

"I do my best," Robert replied.

"Then you'll be an admirable addition to Team Scarab," Sarah said. "I look forward to working together."

Sarah maneuvered past them toward the end of their group, all the pleasantness draining from her features as she approached Amanda Lane.

Amanda tried to move away, but Sarah sidled up next to her.

Their group crossed a quadrangle the size of a football field. Its flagstones were quartz with sparkling veins of amethyst and topaz. It was like walking on rainbows.

---

10. Emperors Constantine and Licinius in 313 C.E. created the Edict of Milan, declaring the Roman Empire neutral to all religions (this to reverse persecution of early Christians). The Edict was later ignored as Constantine heavily *favored* Christians with his policies, laws, and appointments. *Gods of the First and Twenty-first Century, Volume 2, Divine Inspirations*. Zypheron Press Ltd., Eighth Edition.

"I don't recall inviting you onto the team," Sarah told Amanda.

Amanda didn't make eye contact. Her shoulders hunched, and her head lowered as if she were shrinking. "I . . . ," she started. "I was just there, and your cousin gave me a token. . . ."

Fiona wanted to tell Sarah to back off. Amanda hadn't done anything wrong. They were supposed to be on the same side. But she didn't know how to confront Sarah without incurring her anger as well.

Before she could puzzle out the social complexities, Mitch broke ranks and dropped back, walking along the other side of Amanda.

"Did I hear you correctly, Miss Lane?" he asked. "You actually have a scholarship from the League? The League of Immortals?"

Sarah looked over at Amanda disbelievingly.

"It's nothing," Amanda said, trying but failing to keep the hair out of her face.

Fiona was astonished that Mitch had overheard that. More astonished that Amanda was talking about the League in public. Didn't their rules apply to her, too?

"I don't believe Clan Covington has ever received such a scholarship," Mitch said. "Having the blessing of the League, well, that practically makes her a goddess, don't you think?"

Amanda looked up and tried to force a smile on her face.

"Hardly," Sarah said with a snort. She left them, catching up to Jeremy at the head of their group.

Fiona went back to Mitch. "Thanks," she whispered.

"Not a problem." Mitch flashed his easy, reassuring smile. "We're a team, right?"

Before Fiona could tell him that's exactly what *she* had been thinking, Dante pointed to the building on the right: a domed structure that looked like pictures she had seen of the Temple Mount in Jerusalem. This building, however, had a pair of red stone pyramids flanking either side.

"Our main library, the House of Wisdom," Dante told them. "It contains the collection preserved from the Library at Alexandria as well as digitized versions of nearly every book in existence."

Fiona was drawn to the building. So many things she didn't know . . . she could probably spend the rest of her life happily reading in there.

Dante, however, veered away and led them through rose gardens in full bloom.

Fiona inhaled and felt drunk with the overwhelming perfume of flowers.

"Constantine's Court of God's Peace," Dante continued, "was infiltrated by Immortals and secretly used to *preserve* the ancient Pagan ways. The League of Immortals, Infernals, and mortal magical families declared the Court a neutral asset, and since then, the Court continued on in various incarnations. In 1642, it officially became Paxington University in Oxford, England. And at the beginning of the twentieth century, for tax considerations, the campus was finally moved to San Francisco."

Jeremy brazenly plucked an heirloom rose and presented it to Jezebel.

She turned her back on him, ignoring the gesture.

Dante led their group out of the garden.

Jeremy sighed and tossed the flower away.

That was destruction of school property. How could a person like Jeremy effortlessly break all the rules—

while Fiona would have been caught just thinking about it?

They marched into a grove of towering black oaks, redwood, silver birches, shimmering aspens, and willows. A cobblestone path meandered and branched through this peculiar forest.

"Here," Dante said, and waved at the trees, "is the Grove Primeval. The Paxington Arboreal Society imported famous trees from all over the world, many on the verge of being cut down, and replanted them here for safekeeping." He nodded at a few—"the Hangman of London, the Lady in Mourning, Walking Still Spirit"—and then he moved on.

Ahead Fiona saw a building that looked like the Colosseum in Rome, but a tad smaller, and square instead of oval.

Dante continued his lecture. "The Paxington campus appears to the outside world as a prestigious but ordinary private high school. In reality, however, it is where many of the next generation of the world's magical families are trained." He gave an appreciative nod toward Jezebel. "As well as the occasional honor of having a diabolical protégée or Immortal offspring."

Chill bumps pebbled Fiona's arms. Dante hadn't looked anywhere near her when he said this, but it seemed he actually made a point of *not* looking her way. Did he know who she was?

She wanted him to know. She wanted all of them to know.

Just to get a fraction of the attention that Jezebel was getting . . . but there were those League rules, and Fiona knew they wouldn't take her breaking their rules lightly. But hadn't her father said that "everything *was made to be broken* . . . especially *rules*"?

She *knew* she was in trouble if she was even thinking about taking Louis's advice.

"This is where you'll have gym class," Dante said as they approached the archway leading into the coliseum. "The Ludus Magnus."[11]

9

LUDUS MAGNUS

Fiona peered down a long shadowy corridor that led into the Ludus Magnus. She heard distant cheers, angry shouts, and cries of pain. Part of her was afraid and wanted to run away, but part of her was curious and wanted to see.

Dante led the group into the vaulted entrance, through a passage lined with old bricks and ancient stones—even a few skulls and bones had been cemented into the mix.

They came out on a grassy field half a city block wide. In the center sat the most unusual structure Fiona had ever laid eyes on. It was a lattice of posts and crossbeams, a honeycomb of ladders, ropes, and metal poles. It looked like a crisscrossing three-dimensional web spun by an army of mechanical spiders.

---

11. The Ludus Magnus was the name of the Great Gladiatorial Training School unearthed in 1937 C.E. adjacent the famous Roman Colosseum, said to have trained countless professional killers. —Editor.

In the lower part of the structure, a person could barely squeeze through, with sinuous crawlways, tunnels that angled underground, even a canal filled with roaring white water.

Higher, however, the structure was wide open and towered six stories tall with ropes dangling, rickety bridges, and wooden spans barely a handsbreadth wide—which all swayed in the breeze.

"This is the gym," Dante said. "It is part obstacle course and part battlefield. You will learn to hate it by the end of the year. Today four sophomore volunteers will give you a demonstration."

Eliot looked sick.

Fiona moved closer for moral support. This "gym" looked like everything her brother wasn't good at—running, climbing, and dealing with heights.

Four students ran onto the field. They wore sweatpants and sneakers. Two wore red T-shirts; the others wore green. They ran past, giving Team Scarab a polite wave, then halted in front of the gym, eyeing one another with mischievous grins.

Dante clapped his hands. A red and a green banner unfurled at the very top of the structure.

"Winning is simple," Dante explained. "Your team must get half their people to their own flag before the other team gets to theirs. Each team has ten minutes to accomplish this, or *neither* wins."

Dante raised his arms. The sophomores tensed.

Dante dropped his hands. Both two-man teams scrambled onto the lattice and climbed.

"You can take a safer but slower route," Dante said. "Or you can go faster, which is more dangerous."

Fiona saw a green-team student stop climbing about a third of the way up and get onto a narrow beam.

There was only a slender iron pipe alongside to help him balance.

"Aye, there be a bit more to it than that," Jeremy said, and pointed higher.

Two boys were thirty feet off the ground. Both clambered toward a rope swing.

The red-team boy got there first, leaped for the rope, swung around, and knocked the other boy—

—off the platform. The green-team boy twisted and turned through the air . . . bounced off a ladder . . . landed with a thud in the dirt.

Fiona moved toward him, but Dante stepped in front of her. "No interference," he said. "It has to play out."

"Is he—?" Eliot asked, unable to finish his thought.

They watched as the boy who'd fallen slowly got up, his arm hanging at an odd, clearly broken, angle.

"Apparently not," Dante replied.

"You may use *any* means to get to your goal," Dante continued. "And you can use any means to *prevent* your opponents from getting to their goal—short of bringing weapons onto the field."

Fiona thought it a razor-fine distinction between getting kicked off a thirty-foot-high platform and not using weapons. Both were potentially lethal.

Meanwhile, the boy who'd knocked his opponent off swung across a wide chasm, landed, traversed across monkey bars, and then grabbed the red flag.

"Red wins," Dante announced.

"This will be more complicated," Jezebel remarked, "with two eight-person teams. Sixteen participants. The probability for combat will be much greater."

There was a glint in the Infernal's eyes, and Fiona didn't like that one bit.

Amanda Lane, on the other hand, looked so pale now, Fiona thought she might faint.

"Some students," Dante said without looking at any of them in particular, "leave after they see this . . . or after their first match. It is not for the weak of heart."

Fiona wondered how she would do. Lose or win? Grab a flag in glory—or fall into the dirt . . . maybe breaking her neck? She imagined herself climbing and jumping and swinging through the air high off the ground. It made her blood race.

But there was more to this. Maybe Fiona wasn't the smartest here, or the prettiest, nor did she have a clue about the social mechanics . . . but *this* she understood. She could win here and prove to everyone that she belonged at Paxington.

"I can handle this," she said.

"I bet you can," replied Jeremy, who had moved next to her.

The boys climbed down and helped their wounded classmate get up and off the field—even the boy who had knocked him off. There didn't seem to be any hard feelings.

Fiona wondered how much forgiveness there would've been had the boy snapped his spine.

"Well," Dante said. "Any questions?"

"When is our first match?" Sarah asked.

"That's up to your gym teacher, Mr. Ma. He'll probably run you through practice drills first."

Fiona was relieved. She'd need time to thoroughly understand all this and strategize.

Dante led them back to the tunnel and outside.

They took another path through the Grove Primeval, through a particularly dense and dark section of ancient black oaks, and came out on the far side of the quad.

A fountain splashed nearby, and Fiona welcomed

the cooling effect on the warm day. In the center of the water sat a bronze bearded man holding a trident; leaping fish surrounded him—all frozen forever in gleaming metal.

Dante pointed to a row of stately brownstones. "Those are the dormitories for those living on campus." He indicated a larger columned building of gray granite in the distance. "The health center. And over these steps on the hill is Plato's Court, where you'll have most of your freshman classes. "

Robert interrupted. "Hey—what's this?" He pointed back at the fountain.

Two boys stood on opposite sides of the fountain, facing each other across the water. Their Paxington jackets were off, and each held rapiers.

"A freshman duel," Dante remarked. "I supposed I should've covered this. Let's watch."

The tips of their rapiers glistened. One boy was as big as a football player, the other smaller than Eliot . . . even more so because he crouched low.

"Duels are permitted anytime on campus," Dante explained. "But only by mutual consent, of course."

They circled closer toward each other.

The bigger boy rushed his opponent, trying to skewer him through the midsection.

The smaller boy sidestepped and parried—but still stumbled back from the force, and almost fell into the fountain.

"Don't worry," Dante told her, "it's only to first blood."

"But I hear there are always accidents," Sarah added.

Fiona thought it the most barbaric thing in the world. People shouldn't be shoving other people off thirty-foot platforms, and they definitely shouldn't be attacking each other with swords at school.

The small boy parried another attack, riposted—and with a deft twist, skewered the larger boy's hand . . . pushing his blade almost up to the hilt, and then twisting until the larger boy was on his knees.

"See?" Dante said. "Just first blood." He turned away, no longer interested.

Fiona was horrified . . . but couldn't look away.

The smaller boy smiled, accentuating a long scar on one cheek. His opponent was escorted away by two older students.

She wouldn't forget the smaller boy. She might have to face him in gym class.

"Make sure to pick up your reading assignments at the gate," Dante told them, and pointed east. "Miss Westin expects you to be caught up for her first class. You wouldn't want to disappoint her."

"Thanks," Fiona said.

Dante gave her an appreciative nod and then strode across the quad to the library.

"Well," Jeremy said, rubbing his hands together, "we have a fine team. We'll be sure to trounce any competition." As he said this, however, his gaze slid *around* Amanda, as if she weren't there and his description of *fine* didn't apply to someone like her.

Fiona glanced back at the bloodstains by the fountain and then looked over her teammates.

They, in turn, glanced at one another, maybe thinking the same thing she was: Would any of them get challenged to a duel? Would they end up fighting each other? Dante said duels were mutually consensual. No one actually *had to* fight. Or was it trickier than that?

"Yeah," Fiona said. "We're all going to do great."

There was an awkward silence, which Mitch broke. "I don't know about you guys, but I'm getting over to the gate. I've heard Miss Westin assigns a mountain of books the first week."

"We all passed," Sarah said, and casually brushed a hand through her hair. "So what's the worry?"

Fiona had missed almost every question in the magic section on the placement exam. She had a lot of catching up to do.

"I'm out of here." Robert turned and walked toward the gate. He uncharacteristically looked deep in thought.

"Me, too," Amanda murmured, and trotted off to the library.

"We better go," Fiona said, and nudged Eliot. "It was nice—"

Her eyes locked with Jezebel's. It was like staring into clear green water, and drowning. Fiona couldn't quite say it was nice to meet *her*. She had a feeling this girl was going to be nothing but trouble.

She jogged after Robert, calling, "Hey—wait up!"

Eliot came, too. Fiona knew he would, and that was fine because she couldn't leave him alone with *that* group, but she still desperately wanted a few moments alone with Robert. Why couldn't he have figured that out?

Robert had gotten very far ahead of them, although he was just walking. She and Eliot had to sprint to catch up to him as he approached the gate.

Mr. Harlan Dells, the brawny Gatekeeper in the three-piece suit, handed Robert a page-long list of books. Robert scanned it. "I've never read so many books in my entire life," he said.

This was one great difference between her and Robert: Fiona had read almost every book on everything . . . save the one small area of mythology.

Mr. Dells handed her and Eliot their reading assignments. There were titles like *Tanglewood Tales*, *The Golden Bough* (twelve volumes), *The White Goddess*, and *The Hero with a Thousand Faces*.

Even for her, this might take a little time.

"We need to talk," she whispered to Robert.

"I know," he said, and he pretended to still be looking at that stupid list. "I don't know where to start. Things are so weird."

There was something in Robert's voice she had never heard before: doubt. She wanted to take his hand, but that felt wrong in front of Mr. Dells, the man who said he could hear and see almost everything.

"Walk me home?" she asked Robert.

Fiona nudged Eliot, who for once in his life got the hint.

"I think I'll check out that coffee shop," Eliot said, "just to—"

Eliot's mouth was open, but he was no longer talking. He stared beyond the gate.

A black Cadillac with tailfins rolled to a stop just outside.

Mr. Dells growled and moved toward the gate, shaking his head. "You're blocking the entrance. No one is allowed to park here. Not even you. *Especially* you."

"Oh man," Robert said, "I definitely cannot be here." He walked away.

Fiona started after him, but froze as she saw the car door open and the tallest man she'd ever seen get out. His skin was dark. His smile, cold. His eyes locked on to her and Eliot.

Uncle Kino.

"I am not parking," Uncle Kino told the Gatekeeper. "I'm here to pick up. Them."

10

ち

THE GATES OF PERDITION

Eliot stared at the man who climbed out of the Cadillac. Uncle Kino looked taller than he remembered—like he could step over the walls of Paxington, like he was more shadow cast at sunset than flesh and blood.

He blinked and Uncle Kino still looked tall . . . but no longer unnaturally so.

The last time he'd seen Kino, he and Fiona had just been officially accepted into the League. Kino had made a point of shaking Eliot's hand.

"I am here to take them," Kino again told Harlan Dells.

Mr. Dells crossed his arms over his massive chest. "This is a safe haven. They go only if they want to, Mr. Saturday."[12]

Kino sniffed (this might have been a laugh; Eliot

---

12. Kino La Croix (aka Baron Samedi and alternate Voodoo personas, Baron Cimetière, and Baron La Croix. Note: *Samedi* is French for "Saturday.") He is depicted in a white top hat, black tuxedo, and dark glasses. Only rarely seen outside Haiti and other tropical locations. Haitian dictator François Duvalier reputedly dressed like Baron Samedi to increase his air of mystery—although some mythohistorians claim the two *were* the same person (for a while). According to Voodoo practitioners, Baron Samedi stands at the crossroads, where the souls of dead humans pass to the nether realms. *Gods of the First and Twenty-first Century, Volume 5, Core Myths (Part 2)*. Zypheron Press Ltd., Eighth Edition.

wasn't sure) and donned sunglasses. "There's no trouble here today," he told Mr. Dells. "Why don't you go sweep some hallways, eh, janitor?" He turned to Eliot and Fiona. "Come, children."

Audrey and Cee had drilled into Eliot and Fiona since they were little kids that it was very much *not* okay to accept rides from strangers.

But Kino was part of the League. It would be no different if Uncle Henry had come to pick them up. Wouldn't it?

Eliot tried to see Kino's eyes past the smoky lenses of his sunglasses, but couldn't, and suddenly he wasn't so sure.

"This is Council business," Kino explained. "Your mother sent me. She said to tell you that you will be able to do your chores and homework afterward."

Now *that* sounded right. After entrance and placement exams, a campus tour, a reading assignment that probably would take months, and whatever the Council now wanted—of course there would be chores to do at home.

Eliot looked at Fiona, and she slowly nodded, confirming his hunch.

"Okay," Eliot said.

Mr. Dells uncrossed his arms, flipped the switch on the side of the gatehouse, and the large iron gate rolled silently open.

Eliot took a step toward Kino's car.

"Wait." Kino held up his large hand.

"You *just* said you wanted us to come," Eliot told him.

"You got dice on you? No dice!" Kino said, and pushed his sunglasses farther up the bridge of his nose. "Not in my car."

For a second Eliot didn't know what he meant. He

then realized he still had the dice from the Last Sunset Tavern in his pocket. His lucky charms. He'd used them to guess on the last multiple-choice parts of the placement exam he hadn't had a clue about.

He pulled them out of his pocket. "They're just—"

"They're just getting thrown away," Kino declared.

Fiona turned to Eliot and rolled her eyes. That was the look she reserved for when Audrey laid down the law. A look that said, *Shut up and do what you're told, because we're not going to win this one and it's no use trying.*

But Eliot wasn't just going to throw them away. They were his.

He squeezed them in his fist, felt their recessed pips, all those random possibilities contained in his hand. It made him feel in control.

"Toss them here, boy," Mr. Dells said. "I'll hold them for you."

With a sigh, Eliot handed them over.

Mr. Dells rattled them in Kino's direction. The taller man sneered at this and slowly sank back into his Cadillac.

Fiona ran for the front passenger's side door. Eliot sprinted after her.

"The back," Kino told them. "No children up front."

They reluctantly moved to opposite rear passenger doors and opened them at the same time. Eliot paused to admire the way the car's back swept up into two tails.

He then slid inside, and so did Fiona.

The backseats were slick red leather, the interior panels mahogany with chrome accents. There was a smell, not that wonderful new car smell, but more like plastic that had decomposed in the sun.

He and Fiona simultaneously slammed the doors shut.

"Where are we going?" Fiona asked. She nervously plucked at the rubber band on her wrist.

"A short drive to show you children the road ahead," Kino replied. "We want you to make the right decision at the crossroads."

As answers went, this was what Eliot had come to expect from his family: something utterly cryptic.

Eliot eased back and fumbled about for the safety belt. There wasn't any.

"There's no—"

Uncle Kino sped out of the alley and onto the main street without even pausing to look for oncoming traffic.

Eliot and Fiona slid together into the door.

Fiona pushed him away; Eliot elbowed her back.

As he settled back down, he noticed a statuette of the Virgin Mary on the car's dash, her eyes upraised to the pine air freshener dangling from the rearview mirror. All the car's gauges read zero.

They were headed the wrong way to be going home. Instead, Eliot saw the trees of Presidio Park ahead.

"So why no dice?" Eliot asked.

"They are not for us," Kino told him.

"Us? You mean the League?" Fiona asked.

"Dice are an Infernal invention," Kino replied.

"How can that be?" Eliot asked. "Dice have been around forever."

Kino gazed into the rearview mirror. "No good has ever come from dice."

They slowed at the entrance to Presidio Park and turned in.

Eliot had a feeling he should keep his mouth shut, but something bothered him about Kino's distaste for dice. Audrey had a rule for them, too, one curiously devoid of her usual legally verbose wording.

RULE 3: NO DICE.

And when he and Fiona had first been shown to the League Council, they were tested by throwing dice. Everyone had looked so nervous when Henry produced them. What was wrong with dice?

"You've used them before?" Eliot asked.

Kino turned around to face Eliot—no longer even looking where he was driving as he veered onto Lincoln Boulevard. His features could've been molded from cast iron. "No dice," he repeated.

Eliot was used to this stonewall treatment from Audrey. He had his argument ready. "How are we supposed to learn?" he said. "Or make the right choices when we come to this crossroads you're talking about, if no one tells us anything?"

Kino snorted and turned back.

He was silent a moment as he slowly steered the car through the entrance to the San Francisco National Cemetery. Orderly rows of white headstones surrounded them on either side.

"Sure we used the dice," Kino said. "Many, many times in the old days. We loved them . . . too much . . . and made many bad choices."

The Cadillac rolled onto a single lane that turned toward a stand of eucalyptus trees. More headstones and statues of angels appeared clustered in patches of shade.

"The last time we used dice," Kino said, "was after we took the Titans' lands. This was before humans even stepped from the wilderness."

They leaned closer. No one—not even Uncle Henry—had told them about the early parts of their family's history.

Fog swirled through the forest. No big deal in the

Bay Area . . . but it was kind of strange at this time in the afternoon. Strong sunlight shone through in patches and made the mists like veils.

"We had all wanted the land," Kino continued. "We argued, used law and logic—but in the end, there were three who would not bend. Three whom men would later call Zeus, Poseidon, and Hades."

"So you rolled for the land," Eliot said, guessing and inching closer.

More trees crowded this part of the cemetery, plunging everything into shadow.

"Zeus rolled the highest, claiming the kingdoms of sky and earth. Poseidon rolled second highest and took the domain of water." Kino gestured ahead. "I rolled lowest and claimed the shadowy lands that were left as my domain."

The Cadillac eased to stop before a gate. It was simple and small: two-by-fours and chicken wire, something you might put up to keep the rabbits out of your garden.

"We knew Zeus cheated," Kino said, sounding bitter.

He got out and went to the gate.

The gate was some sort of optical illusion, though. As Kino stood by the thing, it seemed as tall now as he was—the chicken wire more solid chain-link and padlocked, too.

Kino opened it with a touch and pushed the gate aside.

He climbed back into the Cadillac, and they rolled past the barrier.

"That was the last time we settled *any* matter with dice." Kino lifted a hand off the wheel and made a sideways cutting motion Eliot knew all too well. Audrey had made that gesture countless times—indicating this conversation was over.

Eliot made a note that Kino was Hades. He'd also remember the names Poseidon and Zeus, two more important-sounding relatives he should keep track of.

He had a feeling there was more to Kino's dislike of dice, and much more to the story of how they related to the Infernals, than he was telling. Eliot felt, however, he'd pressed his luck far enough.

Outside, cemetery headstones packed together so tightly in places, they looked like crooked teeth erupting from the ground; there were statues and monuments side by side so close that no one could walk through.

They rounded another curve, and the headstones thinned and became orderly again and all had military insignia upon them . . . royal crests and crossed swords and eagles in relief.

Eliot looked back. The gate was far behind them, and it had swung shut.

Kino drove up and over a low hill. There were larger structures: mausoleums, obelisks, crude cairns, and something that looked like Stonehenge. There were rolling fields and poplar trees. Sunlight broke through the fog, illuminating wildflowers and making a distant river glisten.

Eliot was positive there was no such river in San Francisco. This reminded him of one of Uncle Henry's lightning-fast journeys across the world. It had that weird dreamy feel to it.

"This is Elysium," Kino said. "Where the noble dead come to dwell for a time."

"So it's another place?" Fiona asked. "Like Purgatory?"

Kino grunted his assent and continued to drive.

So maybe this wasn't like one of Uncle Henry's rides. Kino was taking them to no place in this world. Did that mean *they* were dead now, too? No . . . Fiona had gone to the Valley of the New Year, which she said was part of Purgatory—and she had managed to get back.

He rolled down his window, scared, but wanting a better look nonetheless. Outside, it smelled of fresh earth and rain. Clean.

Eliot set his backpack on his lap. He wanted Lady Dawn close, just in case.

There were people outside. Some sat in marble pavilions talking, painting, or lounging in hammocks. Others gathered about great barbecues, or tossed Frisbees or collected flowers. Couples walked hand in hand.

"All these people . . . ," Eliot said.

"Dead," Kino told him.

They rode past orchards of cherry trees in full bloom that filled the air with feather white blooms, and over terraced hills with row after row of trellises heavy with bloodred and amber grapes.

How could this be? If this was where the dead really came, shouldn't there be *billions* of them here?

Eliot wanted to ask. But he didn't, not wanting to appear stupid.

The Cadillac picked up speed.

Kino touched a button on his door, and Eliot's window slid up.

He turned onto an unpaved branch off the road. The sky was iron gray.

The car accelerated around curves until this road became a single dirt track. The trees became stunted and small, then there were just grass and tumbleweeds, and then just bare rocky dirt. There were no more people here—and definitely no one tossing Frisbees.

Eliot spied a drop-off in the distance.

Kino pressed his foot all the way to the floor, and

the Cadillac leaped ahead, leaving plumes of dust behind.

"What's going on?" Eliot asked.

"Now I will show you the part of the Underworld that belongs to the Infernals," Kino replied, the bitterness thick in his voice, and his eyes glued straight ahead.

Eliot swallowed. That didn't sound good.

The door locks thumped down.

Kino drove and said nothing.

Eliot looked to Fiona, and she gave a slight shake of her head. He wanted to get out, but how? They must be going over a hundred miles an hour—rocketing past jagged boulders—straight toward where the land dropped away.

The Cadillac fishtailed to the left, skating along a cliff—continuing at breakneck speed along its edge.

Eliot slid into Fiona. Neither of them seemed to notice or care; both their faces pressed to the window.

The land plunged more than a mile straight down. A river of molten metal carved through jagged spires of black volcanic rock. In the distance, a desert plain stretched to the horizon. Airplanes, meteors, and flaming debris fell from the sky. Tiny figures swarmed, crowds of people among the rocks and on dunes. They ran, and it looked like they were fighting. Winged creatures circled overhead. One swooped and plucked up a double clawful of people.

Eliot wanted to look away. He couldn't.

"This is what the other family does to the dead," Kino told them. "They torture. Turn souls into wandering insane things. Take a long listen. Remember this next time you hear one of your Infernal relatives and their lies . . . and choose wisely."

Kino rolled down the electric windows.

There was the rumble of distant thunder and volcanoes, and carried on the hot winds were the screams of thousands of lost souls.

Eliot couldn't stand the din. It made him want to scream along with them.

He turned to ask Fiona what she thought, but she was pale and stared straight ahead.

Kino flicked on the Cadillac's headlights. The road they sped along was just a track now through a wilderness of dead twisted trees and whirlwinds of volcanic ash. There was no sun, no stars . . . just darkness.

The Cadillac slowed.

Along the cliff's edge, a fence had been erected. It was giant femurs and rib bones, from dinosaurs, maybe. Concertina wire and long curved talons topped it, pointed away from their side to keep things in Hell from climbing over.

"Why are we slowing?" Eliot asked cautiously.

"The gate is ahead," Kino said without further explanation.

It was the end of the line—literally, as the road curved toward and off the cliff's edge.

Eliot realized one of his hands grasped the leather handle on the back of Kino's seat. He let go.

Mist and smoke parted, revealing a gate the size of their house in San Francisco. It was an interlocked mass of metal and bone and clockwork mechanisms. A half-dozen combination dials sat at eye level. The mass looked utterly impregnable, and like it hadn't been opened in hundreds of years . . . if ever.

"Why would you need a gate here?" Fiona said. "Who in their right mind would want to use it?"

"You would be surprised." Kino pulled up alongside the structure. "Heroes have come looking for lost loves. There are always fools. And the dead are restless." He removed his sunglasses, revealing dark, perhaps sad, but otherwise ordinary eyes. "No one living, not even I, understands what moves them."

The car door locks popped open.

Kino faced them. "This is the Gate of Perdition, where the world of light meets that of darkness. The lands of our family and theirs. When they tell you of the wonders and pleasures of Hell, remember what you've seen here.

"Now," he told them, "get out."

Three heartbeats passed as Eliot and Fiona sat stunned.

"No way," Eliot said.

"I want you to see and hear for yourself first-hand . . . unless you're too scared?"

"I'm not scared," Fiona said. She opened her door and clambered out.

Of course Eliot wasn't scared; his sister was crazy, though, to leave the car.

He sat there a moment, feeling like a total loser and coward. Okay—fine. Eliot couldn't let her go by herself. He opened his door, too.

The only thing that ever felt like this was when he had to open the door to the basement incinerator at Oakwood Apartments. The air was so dry here, it hurt to breathe. He steeled himself, then stepped out.

Kino remained in the car. "Touch the other side," he said. "Feel damnation and the absence of all hope."

"I'm not touching anything," Fiona told him.

Eliot hesitated—but only for a moment. What harm could it do to touch some dirt?

He knelt and wiggled his hand through a gap under the fence.

The earth felt older than anything he had ever touched before. Like it had been dust before the beginning of time . . . totally without life. More dead than dead could ever be.

But it was *not* nothing. Not exactly.

It felt to Eliot more like an empty page: blank, yes, but perhaps the beginning of something. If only the right person would come along, with the right pen . . . they could fill that page up with anything they wanted.

He left the earth where it was and pulled his hand out.

Kino watched him and Fiona. He put his sunglasses back on, and the windows of the Cadillac eased up and sealed with a *thunk*.

Eliot was glad this little demonstration was over.

He and Fiona moved toward the back doors.

The Cadillac's engine revved; the car jumped, fishtailed, and sprayed them with dust.

Uncle Kino sped off.

11

&

BORDERLANDS

Fiona couldn't believe it. "He ditched us!" she cried.

She picked up a rock and chucked it after Kino's Cadillac. It was a futile gesture. The red taillights winked in the distance, obscured by dust and smoke, then swallowed by shadows.

It was very dark. The only light was from a smoldering river of lava in the valley below.

"Eliot?" she whispered.

"I'm here," he said. "Hang on."

He snapped on a flashlight, the same one they'd had in the sewers when they hunted Sobek.

"You're still carrying that around?"

"A first aid kit, too," he said. "Some water, and a few granola bars, just in case. I even have Cee's lunch if we get *really* desperate."

It was one of the few times her brother had impressed her. Fiona would never in a million years, though, tell him this.

Eliot looked through the gate. "Do you really think it's—?"

She stood next to him. Wind blasted her and carried with it a thousand screams and cries of pain from the depths. A plume of magma blasted from a giant fissure and sent a shower of sparks a mile high into the rust-colored sky.

"What else could it be?"

Eliot held up a hand, fingers outstretched. "I feel it's something terrible," he whispered, "but part of me belongs down there. I can't explain it."

Fiona pulled him back from the gate. The heat must have boiled his brains.

"Are you crazy? Nothing *belongs* down there."

But she felt it, too. A little tug . . . as if just on the other side of this valley of nightmares there might be something terrible *and* wonderful, waiting for them. Or maybe it was that feeling you got when you looked down from a tall building or bridge, wondering (but never seriously) what it would be like to jump.

"There!" someone called.

The voice was far away, on the other side of the

gate, and so faint, Fiona wasn't sure if it had been real or not.

It came again, this time more urgent: "A light—I saw a light! Up there! Quick!"

Shadowy shapes scrambled up the steep embankment toward the gate. Men and women, wild eyes gleaming, and carrying with them a scent she'd smelled too many times: on Perry Millhouse, and when Mike Poole dipped his hand into the deep fryer—burned human flesh.

"We better go," she said.

Two figures ran up the path on the other side of the gate . . . then six . . . then dozens.

The ground trembled as they stampeded the gate. They cried and screamed and shouted: *"There! They're opening the gates! Give me that flashlight! You, come here!"*

Eliot backed up.

The gate look impenetrable by anything less than an atomic bomb . . . but the adjacent fence was bone and metal and barbed wire heaped together. Fiona wasn't sure it would stop *all* those people.

She grabbed Eliot's hand and pulled him along faster—running.

A tide of flesh crashed upon the gate and spilled over to the fence. There must be a hundred people pounding on the gate from the other side.

The bones and rusted barbed wire flexed and groaned and shuddered.

And all those people screamed.

The noise stabbed at Fiona's ears. She dropped her brother's hand and instinctively covered her head. It felt like her skull split.

Eliot had one hand over his ear, but the other held his violin and pointed up.

A great bird swooped down from the sky. It was the size of a small airplane: a collection of black feathers and outstretched steel claws and glistening black eyes—and screaming the sounds of breaking glass and nails on blackboard.

The thing tore through the crowd near the gate. There was an explosion of feathers; bone snapped and limbs tossed into the air.

Fiona's heart beat in her throat.

She and Eliot ran.

Behind them, human cries mingled with the bird's and there was a whoosh of wings.

Fiona looked back.

In the glowing sky, the one giant bird disintegrated into a swarm of swirling feathers and claws like a Salvador Dalí tornado of bird parts. It spiraled up and then toward them.

She looked for cover. Eliot's flashlight illuminated a stand of twisted trees ahead, but that was too far away.

Fiona froze—only for a split second, though. She grabbed and stretched her rubber band. The air about its edge hummed as she focused her mind . . . to cut.

"Come and get me," she said. "Just try it."

Eliot stood next to her, his face flushed, and his violin on his shoulder. Bow on strings, he drew out a long, sad note.

The birds hesitated and lost cohesion hearing this—but their momentum still carried them straight toward her.

Fiona braced.

Countless caws and screechings enveloped her. Grasping claws caught her clothes and hair, but failed to find purchase on flesh.

She cut—bone and sinew and feathers—severed even their screams midair.

Behind her, Eliot played: a song of sorrow that bridged to something lighter.

The birds scattered and fell silent before her brother's music. So did the people on the other side of the gate. Even the erupting volcanoes in the distance quieted. Like the entire world paused to listen.

His song spoke of life and love . . . and hope.

Fiona's picked up their flashlight, looking again for cover or a way out of this mess.

There was no trace of Kino's tire tracks in the volcanic ash. The wind had already blown them away. That shouldn't matter, though; all they had to do was follow the cliff edge back the way they had come.

Those birds, however, would come back if they saw them out in the open.

She cast her gaze to the thicket of dead trees. They looked like skeletons with outstretched arms and fingers. Their shadows lengthened and wavered in the beam of the flashlight.

She spotted another flicker of light deep in the forest. Eliot stopped playing.

"Keep going," she whispered. "There's someone, or something, coming through those trees."

Eliot shook his head. "I can't do any more. The song hurts too much." He held one trembling hand to his chest.

That hand of his had never recovered from that infection. Fiona knew he should've seen a doctor. She was about to tell him that he'd been an idiot, but decided now wasn't the time for that. Besides, Eliot looked like he was in real pain.

"It's okay." She looped an arm around her brother and helped him toward the trees. "I think someone's coming to help. And if they're not, I can take care of them."

Fiona wasn't so sure. Her legs were leaden, and the adrenaline that had given her strength before was gone.

She waved their flashlight back and forth.

The light in the forest answered, doing the same.

She and Eliot made their way to the edge of the trees and pushed through until they saw a figure with a lantern. It was all shadow first, and then she saw an arm, a body, a man's rugged face.

She knew him . . . but couldn't place exactly from where. The man looked like a retired athlete, with gray hair and hands that could have grasped a basketball as easily as an apple. He wore camo sweatpants, sneakers, and a black AC/DC T-shirt.

She remembered him then: Their last birthday at Oakwood Apartments, this man had dropped by, just as they had been opening their presents.

"Mr. Welmann?" she whispered.

"Miss Post? It's Fiona, right? And Eliot?" He smiled, but it faded fast. "You're not dead, are you?"

"No," Fiona told him, at first thinking this a stupid question, and then remembering where they where.

Mr. Welmann exhaled.

"We just got here," Eliot said. Her brother had recovered from whatever happened to him back there, because he pushed her arm away and set Lady Dawn back in its violin case.

"I saw that damned Cadillac race past," Mr. Welmann said, "and figured there'd be trouble. Come on. The way out of these Borderlands is back here."

As they started walking, Fiona remembered one thing about Mr. Welmann.

He was dead.

Uncle Henry had told them Audrey killed him to keep the League from finding them. She'd done it with the knife they'd used to cut their birthday cake. It was so creepy.

Eliot asked him, "You called this place the 'Borderlands'?"[13]

"Kind of a demilitarized zone," Mr. Welmann said. He broke through the woods and onto a footpath. He looked around as if he expected someone to come along.

"I don't mean to be rude, sir," Fiona said, "but you *are* dead, aren't you?"

"Sure, kid." He shrugged. "It's not a big deal. We all go sooner or later."

"Our mother—?" she started to ask . . . but couldn't quite articulate the entire question: *Did our mother really kill you?*

Mr. Welmann started up the path and answered, "Yep."

They followed his long strides until patches of sunlight broke through the branches and they heard birdsong.

"I'm so sorry," Fiona said, knowing this could never make up for what had happened. "That's horrible."

"I'm not holding a grudge," Mr. Welmann replied. "I got the impression I'd stumbled into a mother-bear-protecting-her-cubs situation. If I had kids, I might have done the same thing. I hope it turned out all right for you two."

"We're in the League now," Eliot told him.

"And Paxington," Fiona added, pointing to the symbol on her uniform.

---

13. Ye Borderlands be not claimed by good or evil, or anything but whisper and void. Be the wend and winds through the Middle Realms. Shortcut, maze, and dangerous path. Filled with wonders beatific and demonic. Dream and nightmare. Even lost with ye proper guide. Be warned. *Mythica Improbiba* (translated version), Father Sildas Pious. ca. thirteenth century.

Mr. Welmann looked them over, nodding. "Yeah . . . I see it in you now. A spark."

Fiona sensed Mr. Welmann's friendly nature cool toward them.

He led them across a grassy field. Dew soaked Fiona's loafers, but she didn't mind. It was clean, and washed away the volcanic ash.

Mr. Welmann waved at a group tossing Frisbees. He caught one of the flying disks and flung it back. "You must have had some adventures accomplishing all that," he said.

She and Eliot told him everything that had happened that summer: the three heroic trials, the box of chocolates, the return of their estranged father, and the final confrontation with Beelzebub.

Mr. Welmann took it all in without question.

He halted at the top of the hill. Fiona saw the fields stretch out, fading into a distant purple horizon. A river wider than the Mississippi meandered across the plain, seeming from this angle part doodle and part quicksilver reflecting the sky.

"So this is what happens when you die?" Eliot asked. "You come here? And some people go to Hell?"

"I couldn't tell you, kid. I see a few hundred people show up from time to time. The people who go to Hell? I'm happy to say I haven't a clue."

"But that doesn't make sense." Eliot's brows bunched together. "There should be *billions* of people here, then."

"That is *the* question," Welmann said. "Where do they all go?" He knelt, picked a long blade of wheatgrass, and stuck into his mouth. "No one knows. Not me. Not the Infernals." He chuckled. "And certainly not the 'gods.'"

"Someone has to know something," Fiona protested.

"Do they?" Mr. Welmann asked. "Well, the closest thing I have to an answer is that from time to time, the dead move on. Some make rafts and float down the river. Others just start walking." He pointed to the distant horizon. "No one sees them again."

Fiona remembered what Kino had said: *"The dead are restless. No one living, not even I, understands what moves them."*

Welmann sighed. "I feel it sometimes. Don't get me wrong . . . all these barbecues"—he cleared his throat—"the company of fine ladies, and all the leisure time is great. But it feels like there *has* to be something more."

He paused and stared miles away. "I'm not sure what 'more' means . . . Heaven, Hell, or oblivion, but I know there's a final destiny waiting for me."

Fiona sensed the weight and the truth of what he said.

They sat quiet for a moment.

Mr. Welmann laughed and got up. "Geez, that's about enough of that. We better get you two back. If half of what I've heard about Paxington is true, you'll have a ton of books to read your first week."

Fiona nodded.

He led them down the other side of the hill. There were mausoleums and obelisks ahead, and the beginning of the graveyards.

"You know your troubles are just beginning, right?" Mr. Welmann said. "The League is dangerous, and three heroic trials or not, it's never done testing you. The other side of your family won't give up, either. It's not in their nature."

Fiona didn't like the way he talked about the League. *They* were part of the League now. But out of respect for Mr. Welmann, she thought about his warning before she answered.

"The League has our best interests at heart," she told him. "And I think our father has gone away. The other Infernals? No one is going to bother us after what we did to Beelzebub."

"Best interests?" Eliot said. "What about what Kino just did to us? In case you didn't notice—we could have died back there."

They came to a stand of headstones so dense, they had to pick a crooked path through them, single file.

Fiona frowned at her brother's assertion. She wanted to say that Kino just meant to show them what the other side of their family stood for. But what about those people on the other side of the fence who had tried to tear them apart? And those birds? Kino had to know about them. He had to know that leaving them there would be dangerous.

Mr. Welmann lifted a foot onto a headstone to tie his shoelace. "Look," he said, "I'm not trying to scare you. Just decide who you trust and who you don't . . . and watch each other's backs."

Of course that's what they'd do. The question was, whom to trust?

Well, each other, of course.

Her mother? As much as Fiona *wanted* to trust her, Audrey had lied to Fiona and Eliot for the last fifteen years. Maybe for a good reason, but she had still lied. There was no reason to think she wouldn't continue to do so.

"Just over there," Mr. Welmann said. "We're almost to Little Chicken Gate."[14]

---

14. Little Chicken Gate is a rickety structure often mistaken for an abandoned garden or a long-forgotten graveyard. Appearing at random throughout mythohistorical accounts, the gate allows the dead one-way passage to the crossroads that lead them to their ultimate

He slowed. "You two wouldn't know a kid named Robert Farmington? We used to work together. Haven't seen him here yet. I wondered if he was okay."

"Sure, we know Robert," Eliot said. "He's a friend."

"We know him," Fiona echoed, unsure what Robert and she were to each other anymore. He had acted so strange today.

Mr. Welmann, however, did not look happy at this. "He's still driving for Mr. Mimes?"

"Not exactly," Fiona replied. "Uncle Henry fired him. But it's not what it sounds like. He helped us . . . just got into a little trouble with the League."

"He's going to Paxington now," Eliot added.

Mr. Welmann halted and his eyes narrowed. "That can't be right," he said. "No one gets fired from the League and walks away. Robert's a great kid, but he doesn't have the brains or the pedigree to be in a place like Paxington, either. Something stinks. . . ."

"Could he still be working for the League?" Fiona asked. "Watching out for us?"

That would explain his standoffish behavior. As a secret bodyguard, it would be a conflict of interest to get too close emotionally. Her pulse quickened. So it was a forbidden attraction . . . all the more dangerous for them, and exciting.

Mr. Welmann shook his head and started walking again. "The League don't work like that. When they fire you, it's permanent."

"He did mention having to lie low," Fiona said.

---

destinations. For living travelers, however, these rules of transit may be bent, and passage to the nether realms is permitted (although perhaps not desirable), and there is the possibility of *two-way* travel. Extreme caution is urged. The gate can disappear as quickly as it appears. *A Primer on the Middle Realms*, Paxington Institute Press, LLC.

"And when Uncle Kino showed up," Eliot said, "did you see how fast he took off?"

"Do me a favor," Mr. Welmann said. He walked up to the Little Chicken Gate and set one hand on it. "Tell Robert whatever he thinks he's doing, he's in way over his head on this one. Tell him to leave Paxington and ride—just ride. He'll know what I mean."

Despite what Fiona had seen before, the gate was only wooden posts and loose chicken wire strung across their path.

Mr. Welmann opened it for them and gestured them through.

"Thank you," Fiona told him.

"You're welcome, kid. Take care, huh? And don't take this the wrong way, but I hope I don't see either of you again."

She nodded and stepped through.

The sun dimmed. The air felt heavier. Every color dulled.

But this *was* San Francisco. Fiona spotted the paved road and the National Cemetery. It would be a long walk home, but at least they *could* get home now.

She turned to thank Mr. Welmann again for everything.

But although there were footsteps in the grass, and even a little swish where the gate had opened—the Little Chicken Gate and Mr. Welmann were gone.

12

§

HERO-IN-TRAINING

Robert Farmington sat on his Harley Davidson, a curve of blackened steel, dual twin matte black pipes, and the massive V of double cylinders between his legs. The ignition, though, was off, and the bike was in neutral as he rode in the freight elevator to the top of this six-story brick building in the Tenderloin District.

There was no way he was leaving his bike on the street in *this* neighborhood. Not that he could have found a parking spot if he wanted to.

The freight elevator ground to a stop.

This had been one giant hassle of a day—but nothing a ride down the coast, a few cervezas, some fishing, and a long nap in a hammock on the beach couldn't fix.

The elevator door rolled up, and Robert pushed his bike into the loft where Mr. Mimes had told him to meet.

The top floor of this building had been one of those industrial sweatshop operations—now stripped, and in the process of being renovated into a tragically hip and overpriced condominium. Ugly brick walls had been meticulously restored. There were tangles of wiring and computer cables and sophisticated halogen lighting dangling from the rafters. Bluestone tiles made a jigsaw on the floor.

Robert pushed his bike ahead, but halted half in and half out of the elevator.

Aaron Sears was in the loft. He lifted a heavy punching bag onto a hook. He was four hundred pounds of muscle poured into jeans, desert combat boots, and a T-shirt that read BEEN THERE on one side and DONE THAT on the reverse.

Aaron was on the League Council, and had wanted Robert punished for his rule-breaking. Mr. Mimes told them he'd taken care of it . . . but if they found Robert here, unpunished, he was a goner.

Aaron was the Red Rider of the Apocalypse, Ares, the god of war, and half a dozen other aliases—all of them potential trouble and a nasty end for Robert.

He spared a glance at Robert. "I suggest you drag your bike in here, young man, before you lose it."

The elevator door lowered. Robert pushed his bike inside.

The door clicked and locked behind him, and the elevator descended, stranding him.

"Ah, Robert—there you are." Henry Mimes was in the kitchen, hidden by the open stainless steel refrigerator door. He emerged with a bottle of wine and a glass.

"New digs, Mr. Mimes?"

"Do you like it?"

Robert shrugged. His eyes were glued on Aaron.

"Don't worry about him," Mr. Mimes said with a careless wave. Wine slopped out of his glass. "He's here to help."

So, they were all friends now? Robert doubted that.

Aaron released the heavy bag on its hook. The beam overhead creaked. It had to be filled with sand and must have weighed half a ton.

Aaron hit it bare-knuckled. The bag deformed and careened back.

"Where's your Paxington uniform?" Mr. Mimes asked.

Robert had stripped out of the jacket and down to his plain white T-shirt the moment he got off campus. Next order of business was to find some jeans and proper riding boots. He hitched his thumb at his saddlebag, where he had stuffed the blazer.

"It's dry clean only," Mr. Mimes said with a sigh. "Well, no matter. Give us your report."

"Okay, hang on a second. My brain feels turned inside out and wrung dry from the placement exam. I'm glad I only had to do one day of this stuff."

"You *did* have all the answers," Mr. Mimes said, his brows scrunching together with concern.

"Yeah. Those helped. But the answers you gave me weren't in the right order, and guessing which ones went where wasn't easy. Some of the stuff seemed like Greek to me—heck, some of the stuff *was* in Greek."

Robert had cheated under the watchful gaze of Miss Westin. He wasn't sure what she was, but she could give any Immortal in the League a run for their money in the "icy stare" department.

He shuddered.

"And what of the other students?" Mr. Mimes inquired.

"Paxington snobs," Robert said. "Their noses are stuck so far into the air, you've got to wonder how they walk without tripping. Spoiled pukes with a little power inflating their already empty heads."

"As I expected," Aaron grumbled.

"Well, not one girl—that Amanda Lane you wanted me to check out. She's clueless. Made it through her exams somehow, though. I kind of feel sorry for her."

"Ah, good," Mr. Mimes said. "An education is the least we can do for her. The League owes that girl much."

Aaron and Mr. Mimes shared a quick glance.

Robert knew from that simple look there was more to Amanda Lane than they were telling him.

"And the twins?" Mr. Mimes asked.

Eliot and Fiona. A raw nerve twinged in Robert.

He had been glad to see them alive and in good spirits, but the feelings he had for Fiona . . . There was too much there, and it was all so complicated. Robert wasn't built to deal with stuff like this.

"They're fine. Great," Robert muttered. "And, of course, they passed their exams." Robert swallowed, suddenly uneasy. "Only one thing happened at the end . . . Kino." His mouth went dust dry. "He picked them up after school."

Robert was sure he hadn't been spotted by Kino. He'd been just one more clueless Paxington punk in a uniform to him. Robert had gotten out of there quick, though, probably saving himself some fate-worse-than-death League payback.

"Kino moves faster than we thought," Aaron commented. He waved Robert closer.

"Than *you* thought," Mr. Mimes said.

Robert wasn't sure what Aaron had in mind, but he dared not disobey. He moved closer.

Aaron lifted Robert's hands and slipped on light-weight boxing gloves. He indicated that Robert hit the bag.

Robert gave him a *you've got to be kidding* look, but Aaron waited. Robert tried a tentative jab.

The bag was rock solid. Literally.

Aaron frowned, and this made his mustache droop. "With your entire body," he told Robert. "Use your legs. They are your most powerful muscles."

"Now, give me your report from the top again," Mr. Mimes said, "but this time everything about the twins."

Right. The twins. That's what this was all about. Robert was just a spy, a glorified errand boy.

Robert punched. This time he threw his entire weight behind it, and the bag rocked a bit. He shouldn't have been able to do that. He'd never been *that* strong.

Aaron nodded. "Give me twenty like that."

Robert punched as he spoke: "They passed the placement tests. They're both on Team Scarab—the same team I'm on. There's also that Amanda Lane girl on the team. Two from the Clan Covington. One from the Stephenson family. And"—he punched so hard that the bag swung wildly and he had to duck as it came back at him—"an Infernal protégée. A girl called Jezebel."

"Kino is not the only one who moves fast," Aaron said.

"It is nothing unexpected," Mr. Mimes said.

Aaron pushed the punching bag as it swung back— accelerating it to a blur before Robert could react.

It slammed into his face—followed a dizzying moment later by the floor hitting Robert's face as well.

Aaron came over and helped him up, lifting his chin and looking into his dazed eyes. "Should have broken his nose," he told Mr. Mimes. "The Soma appears to be taking."

Robert shrugged off Aaron's hands—got angry for a split second . . . and then cooled down. Getting mad at Aaron, you might as well get angry at a mountain for all the good it would do.

Robert touched his face. It stung, but there was nothing broken. Taking a blow that hard, he should at least have squirted some blood.

"Tell me more about the Infernal," Mr. Mimes said. He had a new glass in his hand, this one with a straw and something that looked like cola inside. He held it out for Robert to sip.

Robert reached for it, but realized he still had on the boxing gloves, so he used the proffered straw.

Whatever it was, it wasn't cola. It was liquid fire and curlicues of multicolored smoke that blasted through his thoughts. It was velvet and honey and a thousand open flowers . . . and sulfur, too, like someone had lit a match under his nose.

Robert exhaled, felt bubbles popping, and the sensations faded.

He'd had this stuff before. Mr. Mimes gave him some when he'd been sprung from that Immortal prison cell.

Was that was Aaron was talking about? What did he call it? Soma? He'd said "the Soma appears to be taking."[15]

"Ah, yes," Mr. Mimes said, noting the quizzical look on Robert's face. "I took the liberty of stocking the refrigerator with a few bottles of this for you. It will do you worlds of good. Now, the Infernal? What did you call her? Jezebel?"

"She's pretty, like you'd expect," Robert said. "Drop-dead pretty, in fact. She had titles . . . Protector of the Burning Orchards, Handmaiden to the Mistress of Pain. Gave me the serious creeps."

---

15. Soma is a ritual drink associated with divinity among early Vedic and Persian cultures, thought to have been prepared from an (as yet) unknown rare mountain plant. Soma is analogous to the mythological Greek ambrosia—what the gods drank and what made them deities (which also appears to have addictive properties). While mortals have struggled for millennia to find the correct plant(s) to brew Soma, and others, most notably the alchemists of Ancient China and Middle Age Europe, have tried to invent the famed Elixir of Life, none have succeeded. It remains an open question if the correct formula can be discovered—or if it *has been* discovered but does not have the desired effect on mortals. *Gods of the First and Twenty-first Century, Volume 4, Core Myths (Part 1).* Zypheron Press Ltd., Eighth Edition.

"Sealiah's minion," Aaron said. "There will be sub-terfuge as well as blood."

"Don't sound disappointed," Mr. Mimes said. "The snakes in the grass will make themselves known soon enough—then you can cut off their heads."

"I don't understand how you know who this Jeze-bel even is," Robert said. "She could be *any* Infernal."

Mr. Mimes cocked one eyebrow. "How so?"

"Well," Robert said, "Lucifer—what did you call it—he 'cloned' me last summer. Made himself look like me to trap Fiona in that Valley of the New Year. Infer-nals can look like anyone they want to, right?"

"No," Aaron said as he pulled on boxing gloves. "Most have only the humanoid and combat forms."

"To be precise," Mr. Mimes added, "only two Infer-nals could ever shift their shape like that: Lucifer and the great Satan. The latter is long departed, his bones dust. And I doubt this Jezebel is Louis in disguise. Even he wouldn't be able to fool the Headmistress and certainly not Paxington's eagle-eyed Gatekeeper."

Robert agreed. That Gatekeeper was an Immortal. Harlan Dells had that look of righteous condescen-sion and unquestionable superiority. It was interest-ing, though, that he wasn't in the League ... or that there could even be Immortals *outside* the League's control.

Aaron approached. He wore boxing gloves now and had his hands up.

"You have got to be kidding," Robert said.

"I don't 'kid' when it comes to combat," Aaron said. "Defend yourself."

He jabbed Robert. It was bullet fast.

Robert sidestepped and swatted the fist away at the absolute last split second. It felt like a steel piston, and would've taken off his head if it had connected.

"Hey!" Robert shouted.

Aaron circled. There was no escape. No way Robert could turn and make it to the elevator.

Mr. Mimes leaned against the wall, watching, and took a sip of wine. "Now, Robert, I want you to tell me about Fiona. How do you *really* feel about the girl?"

"Feel? Wha—?"

Robert never finished the thought. Aaron's fist impacted his gut, squishing the soft bits. Something popped.

There was blackness.

Robert found himself peering through a tunnel, and a high-pitched ringing filled his head. He kneeled, blood streaming from his mouth.

"I said *defend* yourself, boy."

Robert stood.

Slowly stood. But he shouldn't have been able to.

At best, he should barely be able to crawl toward the phone and dial 911 after a sledgehammer punch like that.

"Okay," he said through gritted teeth. He clenched his hands so tight, the knuckles popped.

Aaron came at him again—right and left and straight punches.

Robert intercepted them with strikes of his own. The force knocked him back, but he kept his head down, as Marcus Welmann had taught him.

He kept fighting. Faster and harder.

One of his jabs caught Aaron in his ribs.

Aaron grunted, grimaced . . . and then he smiled.

There was motion—not even a blur, really—just a flicker in the corner of Robert's vision.

. . . When he came to this time, he was flat on his back on the floor.

It felt like his body had been hung up and both Mr. Mimes and Aaron had hammered on it for a few days.

Aaron reached down and hauled Robert to his feet. He turned to Mr. Mimes and said, "He has the potential." Then to Robert, he said, "I shall set up a schedule for you and me to train."

"Excellent," Mr. Mimes said, raising his glass to toast Robert. "Now, Robert, the girl—you're about to tell me how you feel. . . ."

"Oh, man," Robert said, regaining his wits enough to understand what Mr. Mimes was asking. He took a few steps back from Aaron. "Okay. Fiona. I don't know." He felt his insides tighten. "I like her. But it's not that simple. She's in the League."

"Of course it's that simple," Mr. Mimes countered. "You're a boy. She's a girl."

"Yeah, I got that part. But she's a girl who could get me killed."

"How is that different from any other girl in the world?" Mr. Mimes asked. "Do you love her?"

The question caught Robert as off guard as when Aaron had sucker-punched him. "Love?" Robert laughed. "Come on, man. That stuff is for kids!"

There was no way Robert bought into all that. Love was one of two things: what you saw at the movies (fantasies of what girls thought guys should act like); or it was like his mom, who had worked her way through half a dozen boyfriends and stepfathers by the time Robert left home. Even with all the slammed doors, the shouts, the bruises and busted lips—she had "loved" them all.

Any way you sliced it, love was a slippery, dangerous thing.

But Fiona wasn't like any other girl.

There was something more there. She was a goddess . . . maybe . . . and Robert couldn't figure out how that fit into the whole boyfriend-girlfriend thing.

"Yeeeees," Mr. Mimes said. "I see the flames inside you."

Robert shook his head and held up his hands. "Come on, Mr. Mimes. Just tell me what my next assignment is. I need to move, get out of this place."

"Tell him, Henry," Aaron said. "The boy deserves a piece of the truth."

"Hmmmm." Mr. Mimes smiled. "Let me ask you one more thing, Robert. Forget Fiona for a moment. What do you think of Paxington?"

Robert snorted. "It's okay if you like a bunch of stuck-up rich kids and wannabe sorcerers. And if you like book dust and being bored to death in some musty lecture hall. Sure, it's *great*."

"And gym class?" Aaron asked him.

"Cakewalk. I could take those guys without even trying. But like I said, I'm just glad I had to be there only for the one day."

Aaron nodded to Mr. Mimes.

"Robert, my dear boy, I am pleased to tell you that your next assignment *is* Paxington." Mr. Mimes gestured grandly about the half-finished loft. "And this is now yours, along with a generous allowance."

"I don't get it," Robert said. "You want me to set up surveillance on the place? Telephoto lenses and stuff like that?"

Mr. Mimes's ever-present smile faded. "I'm afraid not. This will undoubtedly be your hardest assignment. You're going to go to Paxington. Really go. No more cheating. Musty books, boring lectures, gym class—all of it. You must go for the entire year, Robert. And you must pass."

13

❧

JUST THE START

Eliot walked fast. The sun had already sunk behind the eucalyptus trees in Presidio Park, and the last thing he wanted was a moonlit walk with Fiona through a graveyard.

He just wanted to get home and have this day end.

"You think . . . ," Eliot started. He had a hard time saying it: it was so stupid. "You think that was really Hell?"

"Yes," Fiona replied. "It felt like the Valley of the New Year. Like a dream. But different from a dream, because you felt more awake there."

Eliot nodded.

If their father was Lucifer, he had come from someplace, right? But Hell?

"So there must be a Heaven, too, right?"

Fiona ignored him as she rummaged through her book bag.

Maybe it didn't matter if there was a Heaven or Hell, as Mr. Welmann had said . . . just that there was something else out there, a greater destiny waiting for him.

Or maybe he should stay focused on this world's problems.

Like his hand.

Eliot flexed his fingers. They didn't hurt anymore, but earlier, when he played "Julie's Song" to stop those birds and the people at the fence, the pain had flared so bad, he had to stop. It felt like fire, burning him to the bone. All he'd been able to do for a full minute after that was hold his arm to his chest and let the agony pulse away.

Earlier this summer, a snapped violin string had cut his finger and it became infected.

Eliot, however, no longer thought this was a simple bacteriological infection. There was a connection between the pain and his music. Or maybe the connection was to Lady Dawn. Sometimes when he touched the violin, the infection in his hand felt normal, sometimes even better than normal . . . but sometimes when he played her, it hurt more, too.

Her? Why did people always refer to musical instruments with gender? And why female?

Lady Dawn. This was obviously a girl's name . . . which made sense because he'd always had trouble with girls.

The violin was safely tucked in his backpack, and Eliot was in no hurry to take her out and experiment with what made him hurt and what didn't.

"This is ridiculous," Fiona said. She'd retrieved their Paxington required reading list. She shook the pages at Eliot. "Do you know how long it's going to take us to get through all these?"

Eliot glanced at the list. There had to be a hundred books, and only two—the King James Bible and *Bulfinch's Mythology*—did he recognize from the references they'd seen in other literature.

The rest were probably things Audrey would never have let into their house because of Rule 55, the "nothing made up" rule, which covered books on mythology, legends, and fairy tales.

Despite this rule, however, he and Fiona *had* learned things—from snippets of overheard conversations, people on the radio, and bumper stickers. Things like, HAVE FAITH IN GOD, THE DEVIL MADE ME DO IT, SINNERS AND DEMOCRATS BURN IN HELL, and WALK GENTLY ON MOTHER EARTH.

"It's like her entire plan to keep us 'safe' totally backfired," Fiona said as if she were reading his mind.

"That's why she's sending us to Paxington," Eliot said. "To fill in the blanks."

"More like *we* get to make up for *her* mistakes."

They turned the corner. The entrance to Paxington should have been just down the street, but he couldn't see it yet—not that Eliot had any desire to go back to school today. He just wanted to rest after this too-long, dangerous, and completely weird day. Still, it was fascinating that the entire campus was close: tucked in some in-between place in the middle of San Francisco.

A black cat sat in a doorway, staring at them. When Eliot met its amber gaze, the cat looked away, preened itself, then left, tail flicking in irritation.

"Maybe," Eliot said, "it doesn't matter anymore who, if anyone, is to blame. What's the point? We've got homework to do tonight. We should concentrate on that."

"It should matter," Fiona said. "Why are you always so eager to please her?"

"Me? You're the prenatal *Vombatus ursinus*."[16]

Fiona pursed her lips and slowed. She knew exactly what he had meant—that she was tied to Audrey like some suckling baby. Not adult enough to make her own decisions.

---

16. *Vombatus ursinus,* the common or "coarse-haired" wombat. The wombat is a marsupial indigenous to the cooler, wetter regions of Australia. They gestate a single offspring (a *joey*), which spends nine to eleven months within its mother's pouch. —Editor.

"At least," she said. "I'm big enough to come out of the pouch."

Eliot halted in his tracks. That wasn't playing fair. Vocabulary insult was about clever etymologies and double entendres, not simple putdowns like that.

And besides, he was only an inch or two shorter than she.

Eliot didn't feel like playing vocabulary insult. He walked ahead of her.

Fiona trotted up to him. "I'm sorry. I didn't mean that."

"Whatever," he said.

Eliot glanced across the street, still not seeing Paxington where it should be—then in a flash, the alley aligned and tunneled to fill his vision. Eliot got a glimpse of the café and older students chatting at tables under a blue canopy decorated with a river of glowing stars, sipping coffee, and reading books or scrolls. Beyond this he saw the gate. Mr. Harlan Dells was standing there, arms crossed over his chest, smirking as if he had eavesdropped on him and Fiona.

Streetlights flickered on, and Eliot blinked.

The slice of sideways reality extending into Paxington vanished.

Seeing his new school reminded Eliot there were plenty of other things to worry about besides a reading assignment. That would be the easy part.

"What are we going to do about gym class?" he said. "It looks like a person could get seriously hurt."

Fiona marched alongside him awhile before she answered. "Don't worry. I'll watch your back."

"So you think *I'm* going to need watching? You think I'm helpless?"

"No." She glanced at him, and then at his backpack. "Far from it."

There was a tentative quality to her voice that Eliot had heard only rarely . . . as if she was scared.

Eliot quickened his pace. He didn't want to think about why his own sister would feel that way about him. It wasn't like *he* had conjured a fog filled with the dead or made the sun rise early on command. That had been the music, out of control—not him.

"I just meant that we're a team," Fiona said. "And people on a team watch out for each other. That's all."

They rounded a corner, turning onto their street. Even though it was still a block away, Eliot spied the highest window in their house. A candle burned there, a beacon for them. Cee must have lit it.

"I don't think Jeremy or Sarah Covington are concerned about being team players," he said.

"At least they know how things work at Paxington," Fiona replied. "We can learn from them. I'm more worried about that Jezebel."

The Infernal. The Julie Marks look-alike.

"You've got that stupid look on your face," Fiona said, "like you think she's going to date you." She shook her head. "Listen, she's dangerous. We just walked back from the brink of Hell—that's where people like that come from. She's evil. Stay away from her, okay?"

Eliot stopped and crossed his arms. "We're part Infernal, too. Does that mean we're evil?"

"We're Immortals," Fiona told him. "The League said so."

"Then why did Kino make such a big deal about telling us we might have a choice? Why drive us right to the Gates of Perdition and ditch us? He was obviously trying to scare us into choosing his side."

Fiona considered this.

"Maybe . . . ," she said, and she started walking again.

"Don't worry about Jezebel," Eliot told her. "It's not like she's even noticed me."

"True," Fiona said with a hint of sarcasm.

She didn't have to agree so easily. "So, what's the deal with you and Robert?" Eliot shot back.

"That's none of your business."

"Sure it is. He's on our team now, isn't he? I thought you two were, I don't know, closer."

Fiona sighed. "We were. But now I don't know what to think. He got into trouble because of us before. Because of me. If he gets noticed by the League . . . you know what they'd do to him."

They turned off the sidewalk and mounted the stairs of their porch.

Cee opened the door and beckoned them inside. "Come in, my darlings! Congratulations! We ordered Chinese to celebrate your first day, and we wouldn't want it to get cold." She trembled with excitement. "I'm so glad you passed all your tests."

Eliot glanced at Fiona, sharing a quizzical look. Cee already knew how they did on their tests?

Of course they knew. Audrey would have called Miss Westin.

They followed her inside, and Eliot detected the savory scents of Mongolian beef, five-star golden shrimp, and pot stickers.

He and Fiona dropped their bags and raced upstairs.

On the dining table were white cardboard boxes overflowing with noodles and rice, steaming vegetables and dumplings. Eliot and Fiona grabbed plates and piled the food high.

Eliot devoured one entire plateful, went back for seconds, and then finally looked up.

Cee watched him and his sister with rapt attention. "Tell me everything," she said.

Eliot wanted to tell her about the exams, how Paxington was hidden in plain sight, the duel they saw, and the students he'd met. It was all so different—scary and wonderful . . . mostly scary.

But what to tell her about Uncle Kino, their drive to Hell, getting ditched, and then Mr. Welmann's—the dead Mr. Welmann's—timely rescue?

Cee knew about school already. She might even know about Uncle Kino.

But the stuff Mr. Welmann had told them about what happened to the dead . . . that somehow seemed like a secret.

He glanced at Fiona.

She'd had eaten only a few morsels off her plate and was in the process of pushing the rest around. She looked up. She narrowed her eyes slightly to let him know they had better keep that information to themselves . . . at least until they had a chance to figure it out.

"It was great," Eliot told Cee. "But we're beat and we have tons to read tonight."

"There's this list of books," Fiona chimed in. "You wouldn't believe it."

"You were late," Cee said. "We weren't sure what happened to you."

Eliot felt like he'd been stuck with a pin, and he sat up straight.

Cecilia's words were wrong. On one level, they were just normal words like he'd heard a bazillion times before from her . . . but there was also an undertone: reflected mirror images of words, shadow words, whispered backward and upside-down words.

They were *lies*.

Cee knew exactly where they had been.

Eliot didn't know how he knew—but he was sure she wasn't telling the truth.

Why would Cee pretend not to know? Just to get more information out of him?

Well, two could play that game. Eliot's gaze returned to his food, and he prodded a dumpling with his chopsticks. He didn't answer her question; instead, he asked, "Have you heard anything from our father? I mean, since Del Sombra? I thought he'd have called or written . . . or something."

"Of course not," Cee said. "There's not been a single word from the scoundrel. And we're lucky for it."

Eliot discerned only the truth from her words that time.

"But he is going to show up again, isn't he?" Fiona asked.

Cee licked her lips, gently patted Fiona's hand, and replied, "I know he is your father, my dove. You must have feelings for him, but best to let them go."

A shadow appeared in the stairwell, and Audrey spiraled down from her upstairs office. She carried a cigar box in the crook of her arm. "Good," Audrey said, "you're finally home." She settled at a table and poured herself a cup of green tea. She took a sip, all the while watching them, and then said, "I'm very proud of you both for passing the entrance and placement examinations."

That wasn't what Eliot had expected. He and Fiona had received Cs on that placement exam. Well, he got a C+. In this household, the *only* passing grade was an A.

"I spoke with Miss Westin," Audrey said. "She was impressed with you . . . considering the challenges we had with your homeschooling."

"Challenges?" Fiona dropped her chopsticks.

Before Fiona could start protesting, though, Audrey cut her off. "I see you have the reading list." Audrey nodded at the pages near Fiona. "Two sets of those books are being delivered by courier this evening. I didn't want either of you to wait another instant to make up for lost time."

Fiona reddened.

Audrey continued, holding out her hand to forestall her. "I know what you're going to say—the lies, the deliberate obfuscation of our family's history, and how it is 'not fair'—and then I would tell you it was for your own good, and life is never fair, and that we should focus on our present duties. So, let us imagine we've already covered that well-trodden territory, so I may give you your gifts."

Fiona blinked.

Eliot didn't understand. Their dangerous journey today seemed almost par for their new lives. And the mountain of reading they'd have to do seemed right, too. But Audrey accepting a C on tests? Even being proud of them? And now presents on a day that wasn't their birthday?

That was just plain weird.

Audrey said to Cecilia, "Go prepare dessert."

"Oh yes, yes." Cecilia said, and backed toward the kitchen. "Yes."

"And," Audrey called after her, "do not *add* anything to it." She turned back to Eliot and Fiona. "It's ice cream and cake from the Whole Foods Market."

She opened the cigar box she had carried down. Audrey removed two cards, setting one before Fiona, and then Eliot.

He stared into the card's gleaning stardust platinum surface. It had raised numbers and in capital letters, his name: ELIOT Z. POST. He'd seen these before, working at the pizza parlor, but he never believed he'd have a real credit card himself.

Audrey handed him a ballpoint pen. "Sign the back," she said. "That's very important."

Eliot obeyed, and then handed the pen to his sister. Fiona looked dumbstruck.

"You'll need a thousand little things for school," Audrey explained. "More books, clothes, athletic equipment, or the occasional snack. You are to use these for all your expenses."

Eliot picked the card up. It seemed heavier than plastic, like maybe it was real platinum.

"These cards are financially backed by the League," Audrey told them, her voice solidifying into its normal somber tone. "I therefore expect you to use them responsibly."

"We could buy anything?" Eliot asked.

"If you need," Audrey said. "Yes."

Before, Eliot always had to scrape together spare change just to buy some juice. Limitless money? It seemed like another test. Like that never-ending box of chocolates his sister had gotten.

"There is a number on the back of the card," Audrey told them. "Call it if the cards are lost or stolen. It is also the number to call if you need to contact the League for any emergency. Program it into your phones tonight."

From the cigar box she removed two contoured black shapes and gave one each to Fiona and Eliot.

It easily fit his hand, and his thumb naturally found a recessed button. He pressed it, and the shape clicked open. There was a tiny keyboard, a number pad, and computer screen that lit up.

"I understand that no respectable teenager today is

without one of these contraptions," Audrey said. "I left the phones' instruction manuals in your rooms."

"Wow!" Eliot breathed. "Thanks, really!" He got up and gave Audrey a hug.

"Thank you, Mother," Fiona said. She got up and gave Audrey a hug as well.

"Now, go wash up." Audrey brushed volcanic ash from Fiona's skirt. "I cannot believe Cecilia allowed you to the dinner table in such a filthy state."

Eliot and Fiona obeyed and ran to the bathroom.

Fiona got there first, and started washing her hands.

"This is great," Eliot told her as he examined his new phone.

"Don't be a dork," she replied, scrubbing her face.

"What's your problem now?"

"We wouldn't be getting all these things unless we're going to need them," Fiona said. "Unless there was *real* trouble coming. Like our heroic trials this summer. Paxington, the League, our father's family—Mr. Welmann was right: This is going to be a lot harder than we thought."

The happiness drained from Eliot.

His sister was correct. Today with the tests, that preview of gym class, the duel they witnessed, and the ride to Hell and back—all that had happened on their *first* day of high school.

With a sinking feeling in his stomach, Eliot realized that ahead of him was an entire year of days like this.

II

RIGORS OF
ACADEMIC LIFE

14

❧

BLOOD PEDIGREE

Fiona and Eliot strolled into the Hall of Plato. One hundred and twenty-six students, the entire freshman class of Paxington (minus themselves), filled the amphitheater seating of the classroom. The gaslights were lowered. It smelled of chalk dust and old books.

Miss Westin stood upon center stage and peered at them over her glasses. Her gaze chilled Fiona to the bone.

Heads turned their way, and everyone whispered.

"Master and Miss Post," said Miss Westin. "How good of you to join us again." She stepped to the lectern, opened a black book, and made two marks.

There had been some confusion this morning because Eliot's rusty alarm clock had finally busted, and the grandfather clock in the dining room had been sent out for cleaning. Fiona could have sworn they were an hour *early* . . . which was why they had dawdled, wandering the halls of Paxington, admiring the murals and mosaics that covered the walls. The ones in Plato's Court showed gods, their battles, and wondrous pastoral scenes with eighteenth-century ladies in flowing dresses.

"Find a seat," Miss Westin said. She turned to black-boards suspended by chains from the ceiling. They were covered in her perfect cursive script, and one board had the title, *Origins of the Modern Magical Families (Part One).*

Fiona looked for seats. There were concentric circles of fold-down seats and desks, but all were taken.

In the dim light, she saw Mitch Stephenson and Robert; either boy, she bet, would have given up his seat . . . which would have been nice, but she didn't want to make any more of a scene than they already had.

"They're all full," Eliot whispered. He donned his glasses and looked around the lecture hall. "Should we stand in the doorway?"

How humiliating. Their first real class, and already they looked like total dorks.

"I guess so. . . ."

As she turned, however, Fiona spotted Jeremy and Sarah Covington waving to her. They pulled off backpacks and jackets they had set in adjacent seats.

"Ugh . . . ," Eliot said.

"Don't be that way. Come on."

She clambered down toward the Covingtons, but hesitated. Did she sit next to Jeremy, who had once tried to kiss her? Or next to Sarah, who, for some reason, intimidated her even more than Jeremy did?

Jeremy patted the seat next to him and smiled.

Fiona sat next to Sarah (who scooted away from her).

"Thanks," Fiona whispered.

"You are most welcome, teammate," Jeremy said.

Eliot and Jeremy exchanged awkward smiles, and then Eliot took the seat by him.

"About time," said the boy in front of them, clearly annoyed by this disruption.

"Shhh." Jeremy's stare bored into the back of the boy's head.

Miss Westin cleared her throat. "Before we start our lecture on the modern families, we shall review the origins of various magical lines."

She pulled down a section of blackboard, revealing a gorgeous illustration of an oak tree in cross section—like those diagrams showing the evolution of protozoa, dinosaur, bird, chimpanzee, and finally modern man.

In this diagram, however, Fiona saw leaves and intricate wood grain, and upon the tips of the upper branches were neatly printed names, and on the lower branches Greek symbols, cuneiform . . . and then older unrecognizable symbols.

"The ancient forces," Miss Westin lectured, "the Old Ones, the gods, Infernals, and the Fey—these are our murky past, and much of what we know of it are lies. As you review the texts, note the obvious embellishments and question all 'truths.'"

She gestured at the lowest branches, the ones gnarled and clearly dead. "We merely mention the existence of the Primordial Ones from before time. All are dead or forever banished—incomprehensible now and forevermore to mortals and Immortals alike. We leave their delicate and dangerous studies for your junior and senior years."

The symbols on those lower branches were lines and dots and tangles of geometries that compressed to points as Fiona stared at them. She felt suffocated—strangled. She blinked, and the symbols were once more flat and plain chalk.

She should be writing this all down. Fiona fumbled out her notebook, accidentally nudging the boy in front of her.

The boy turned around. "Do you mind?" He was

pale; his hair, dark and straight and falling in a neat angle across his glare.

"I'm so sorry," she whispered.

"Eyes up front, cad," Jeremy spat back.

The boy snorted, but nonetheless turned back to face the lecture.

Fiona's face burned. She was glad she was in the shadows. She nudged Eliot so he, too, could take notes, but his eyes were riveted on the blackboard to where Miss Westin next pointed.

"The Titans," Miss Westin said. "Their origin and connection to the Old Ones is murky at best. This branch, with one notable exception, is now extinct."

Fiona squinted. She read crossed-out names on that branch: Oceanus, Hyperion, and Tethys. The one not crossed out was Cronos, the Harvester, Keeper of the Sands of Time, founding member of the League of Immortals, aka Cornelius Nikitimitus.[17]

Uncle Cornelius? The frail old man on the Council was one of the oldest living things in the world?

Fiona scanned the other names, followed a side branch, and her breath caught in her throat as she read: (Son of Iapeuts) Prometheus, Bringer of Fire, aka Perry Millhouse.

Perry Millhouse had been a Titan, too. Nausea rolled inside her as she remembered how it had felt to cut through him.

"The Titans," Miss Westin continued, "were the

---

17. Cronos the Titan is often differentiated from the Chronos, the Greek deity and personification of Time. Modern mythohistorians, however, now believe they were the same entity, this later persona created for Cronos when he joined his offspring in their rebellion against the ancient Titans. *Gods of the First and Twenty-first Century, Volume 4, Core Myths (Part 1).* Zypheron Press Ltd., Eighth Edition.

progenitors of many of the gods of the prehistoric and classical eras. Their children rose up to challenge them, recruiting some to their cause—but in most cases eliminating their parents altogether."

Fiona's mouth dropped open, horrified. Uncle Henry, her mother—they had *murdered* their own mothers and fathers? Was that what they were afraid Eliot and she might do one day? Was that the reason Immortals treated their offspring so badly? Because they were afraid of them?

"This transition from Titan to the Immortals," Miss Westin said, "occurred circa eight thousand years B.C.E."

That was *ten thousand* years ago. They were all so old. Fiona felt suddenly insignificant. Was that what she glimpsed when she looked into her mother's eyes? The experience and knowledge of millennia judging her fifteen years of attitude and arrogance?

She searched the next branch—the Immortals—and found two familiar names: Hermes, messenger/spymaster for the League of Immortals, aka Henry Mimes; Ares, League of Immortals Warlord, aka Dr. Aaron Sears.

There was another branch next to this—connected only by a dotted line and punctuated by a question mark.

On this offshoot were three names: Atropos, Lachesis, Clotho.[18]

---

18. The three Moerae, the Norns, or the Fates are Clotho, the youngest Fate, who spins the thread of a person's life; Lachesis, the middle Fate, who measures the length of a person's life; and Atropos, the oldest Fate, who cuts the thread of life. Their origin is unclear. In many accounts, they are the daughters of Zeus; in others, they are the daughters of Nyx (the primordial Goddess of Night). As Norns, the three are described as maiden giantesses who simply arrived in the hall of the gods in Asgard and marked the end of the

"Atropos," Fiona whispered to Eliot. "Audrey . . . Post."

He nodded.

She wanted to ask Miss Westin what that dotted connecting line meant. Fiona started to raise her hand, but she hadn't seen anyone else interrupt the lecture. She'd wait until the end of class.

Miss Westin indicated another branch. This one coiled up from the base, a snaking vine with a dozen names, like Sealiah, Leviathan, and several that had been crossed out, such as Satan and Beelzebub (which sent shivers down Fiona's back).

One name was most peculiar in that it had been written, crossed out, and then rewritten: Lucifer—the Prince of Darkness, the Morning Star, aka Louis Piper, her father. . . .

"The Infernals are the exception to the preclassical cutoff date for living immortal beings," Miss Westin explained. "Many of the fallen angels are still active in their Lower Realms . . . and occasionally venture to the Middle Realms as well.

"Other immortal branches"—Miss Westin gestured to a half dozen others, grayed out—"the Fairies or Folk of the Aire, the King's Men, Atlanteans, and the Heavenly Angels are all thought dead or departed."

Jeremy leaned over Eliot's lap, closer to Fiona. "The Fairies be hardly gone," he said. "I've seen them—chased the little buggers, even held their gold. That's how I came to find myself in the Valley."

---

golden reign of those gods. Whatever their source, it was soon proved that they held the (not-so) metaphorical threads of fate for *both* mortals and Immortals. Even the gods feared the Fates. *Gods of the First and Twenty-first Century, Volume 4, Core Myths (Part 1).* Zypheron Press Ltd., Eighth Edition.

Sarah sighed as if she had heard this a hundred times.

Fiona nodded to be polite, but she really wanted to hear Miss Westin's lecture, and wished he would shut up.

"Now," Miss Westin said, "on to the *mortal* magical families."

. She pulled down a section of the adjacent blackboard. On it was a detailed expansion of the younger, topmost branches with dozens of names, including Van Wyck, Covington, Kaleb, and Scalagari. There were also more cryptic titles like "The Dreaming Families" and "Isla Blue Tribe."[19]

"The thing about Fairies," Jeremy continued to tell Fiona, oblivious of the lecture, "is that they didn't want anyone to know they're still alive. They had it in for me because I knew. Lured me with a trail of gold . . . just to shut me mouth. What they didn't know was—"

The pale boy in front of them turned and quietly but firmly told Jeremy, "Too bad they couldn't keep it shut, Covington. Close your piehole, before I close it for you."

Jeremy considered this threat, and his lips curled into a cruel smile.

"Here we go," murmured Sarah. She closed her notebook and set down her pen.

Jeremy eased back in his seat and held up both hands. "Of course, laddie. My apologies."

---

19. There are two dozen major, and a score of lesser, mortal magical families. Among many interests, they control global pharmaceutical conglomerates, diamond mines, crime syndicates, and political infrastructures. Although nowhere near as powerful as the Infernals, or as influential as the League of Immortals, they collectively control one twelfth of the world's assets. *Gods of the First and Twenty-first Century, Volume 14, The Mortal Magical Families.* Zypheron Press Ltd., Eighth Edition.

The boy glared at him a moment and then turned back to the lecture.

Jeremy picked up his copy of *Bulfinch's Mythology*—and slammed it into the back of the boy's head.

The boy reeled forward, scattering his papers onto the floor.

Fiona was stunned. She knew there could be fights at Paxington; she'd seen that duel the very first day . . . but in class?

Miss Westin clapped her hands once. That instantly got the entire room's attention. Even the boy who'd been clobbered looked at her, and didn't move or say a word.

Miss Westin took a deep breath and in an even voice said, "Mr. Covington, Mr. Van Wyck—if you have differences to work out, do so outside my classroom." She looked them over a moment, a gaze that reminded Fiona of glacier ice, utterly cold and unstoppably crushing. "I sense your blood is up, however, so the lecture will be suspended for ten minutes. Resolve this. Now."

"Suits me perfectly," Jeremy said, and stood. "This Van Wyck cad should be taught some manners, using such language before a lady." He gave a quick bow in Fiona's direction.

Fiona pushed herself deeper into her seat. She felt as if everyone were staring at her.

Jeremy hit him on her account? Or was that just an excuse?

The other boy got up.

Although he was on a lower row in front of them, he stood taller than Jeremy by a full head and was so bulky, it looked like he could, and would, pick up Jeremy with one meaty hand and crush him. "Okay, Covington, you're on." He stalked out of the lecture hall.

Jeremy pushed past Fiona. Sarah got up to follow her cousin.

So did Eliot . . . and then Fiona . . . and then everyone in the class.

Outside they all crowded about Jeremy and the Van Wyck boy. Looking at the ludicrous size difference between the two, Fiona was seriously worried Jeremy was going to get killed.

The Van Wyck boy looked down on Jeremy, pausing . . . because perhaps he was wondering what it would prove to beat up someone in such a mismatch?

"Why don't we forget about this," the Van Wyck boy offered. "There's no point in fighting. Unless you were going to use only magic."

Robert Farmington sidled up next to Fiona. At first she didn't recognize him in his neatly pressed school uniform. He had gotten a haircut, too.

"I've been wanting to talk to you," Robert whispered to her.

"Me, too," she said. "But now's not the time."

"Right."

Robert sounded disappointed. But how did he expect her to talk when Jeremy was about to get pounded flat?

Jeremy stuck his face a hand's span from the other boy's. "You want to see me magic? Well, here's some."

Jeremy spit into his face.

The Van Wyck boy turned red. He stepped back, cleaning off the spittle with one quick angry wipe. "Okay, Covington—you asked for it!"

Jeremy backed off, smiled, and danced back and forth as the other boy started shrugging off his jacket.

Jeremy didn't wait. He socked him in the nose.

Bone and cartilage cracked.

The Van Wyck boy fell backward into the wall, both hands covering his face, tears gushing from his eyes.

The students cheered and yelled.

Jeremy punched him in the gut. He lashed out with his foot, connecting with the other boy's knee.

The Van Wyck boy doubled over. His leg crumpled.

Jeremy kicked him once, twice.

Fiona felt something greasy in the back of her throat and thought she might be sick.

Miss Westin watched impassively, arms folded over her chest, almost as if she were grading the boys on a test.

If no one was going to stop this—Fiona would.

She pushed her way through the crowd.

Jezebel, though, got there first. The other students let her pass, seeming to fear getting in the way of an Infernal. She stepped between Jeremy and the Van Wyck boy just as Jeremy brought back his foot for another kick.

"You've won," Jezebel said.

Jeremy blinked, and the rage faded from his eyes. "Do you think so?" He drew back, smiling, for one final coup de grâce.

"First blood"—Jezebel nodded to the downed boy—"is as far as they allow in campus duels."

Jeremy lost his smile as he watched his opponent cough a globule of blood and snot from his face.

"Continue if you want," Jezebel nonchalantly told him, "but it would be a shame to have a team member suspended over such a trivial rule." She glanced at Fiona. "And over such a *slight* reason."

Jeremy straightened his jacket and brushed back his silky blond hair. He knelt and told the boy, "That should teach you a lesson. Next time, mind your manners when in the presence of a lady."

Jeremy then bowed to Fiona, and although he faced her, he seemed to be performing for the watching crowd. "Your honor be upheld, fair maid."

A few girls giggled.

Fiona wanted to slap Jeremy's grin off his face . . . but there'd been enough violence for one day.

Miss Westin, without comment, turned and marched back to class. Most of the students took this as their cue to leave as well.

Fiona went to the Van Wyck boy to help him up, and even though it wasn't her fault, she thought she should apologize.

The boy's bloodshot eyes stopped her cold, however; it was pure spitting-cobra venom.

He blamed her. And there'd be no explaining or apologizing it away.

Fiona also knew that somehow, one day, he was going to get even with Jeremy . . . and with her.

15

THE TRUTH WILL HURT

Jezebel stepped off the Night Train, slipped off her loafers, and set her bare feet upon the black loam of the Poppy Lands of Hell.

She wriggled her toes, felt her blood pulse, and felt the warmth and life flow back into her bones.

Although she wore the uniform of a Paxington

schoolgirl (not the pantyhose, however; there were limits to what she would endure), and although she looked much like a mortal girl (albeit one of extraordinary and enchanting beauty), within her heart beat pure poison and hellfire.

She was Infernal. This was her domain.

They belonged to each other.

Jezebel inhaled the pollen-laden air, tasted the odors of vanilla and honeysuckle, the sweet decay and mold spore.

Behind her, the train hissed and screamed and pulled out of the station house.

Jezebel picked up her book bag and strolled to the adjacent stables.

Servants bowed and scraped before the Duchess of the Many-Colored Jungle and Handmaiden to the Mistress of Pain.

They handed her the reins of the readied Andalusian mare.

The snow-white beast neighed, stomped with razorshod hooves, and then bowed its head as well, recognizing her status.

Jezebel mounted, wheeled about, and galloped toward the Twelve Towers to make her report.

The Poppy Lands lay in perpetual twilight. Luxuriant fields of color spread in all directions; opium flowers and orchids looked like a galaxy of fallen stars. Between thunderous hoofbeats, she heard the endless churning of worm and cockroach through the rich soil. In the distant hills rose the jungle, thick and dark, covered with vines and moldering with resplendent fungus.

She dimly remembered what it was to be mortal in this realm, and she recalled being repelled by the narcotic decay and the overwhelming vapors.

This was a dim memory, though—the vestiges of her hope-filled human soul.

It hurt to remember.

Her Queen had told her if she ignored it, it would soon go away—like the summer sniffles.

Indeed. She was Jezebel now, filled with the power of Hell, primordial and more intoxicating than the opium to which she had once been so addicted.

The serfs of the fields genuflected as she rode past.

They did not tend to the poppy harvest as usual, but rather cultivated spear and pike thickets, rolled spore cannons upon the backs of the giant bats as the animals hissed and squeaked in protest, and propped suits of plate armor among the twining bramble . . . which would coil and fill them and bring them to life.

As she neared the cliffs of the Twelve Towers, she saw engineers strengthening its fortifications. Antiaircraft artillery squatted upon the ramparts. The walls were heavy with creeping death vines, which bristled with thorns and oozed a flesh-corrosive toxin.

Even the land prepared for inevitable war. The Laudanum River that wound through the valley rainbowed with oily slicks as the jungle that had overgrown its banks wept poison to make it a moat of death.

Jezebel clattered up the cobblestone road and through the castle's raised portcullis.

Guards in thorn armor and flower-laden lances saluted her and helped her dismount. The Captain bowed and indicated the Queen awaited her pleasure in the Chamber of Maps.

She raced up the stairs of the Sixth Tower, the so-called Oaken Keeper of Secrets.

It was not wise to keep the Queen waiting. Ever.

She paused outside the chamber to adjust her skirt

and smooth her Paxington jacket, to make sure her hair was just right.

Jezebel sensed Sealiah near. They were connected through the Pact of Indomitable Servitude, the oath that broken and damned Julie Marks had taken to transform herself into Jezebel. It made her a part of Sealiah's will, Julie's soul consumed and replaced by the shadow of the Queen of Poppies. Jezebel felt this in her very atoms. She did not struggle against it. One might as well try to struggle against breathing.

She entered the chamber, bowing low, not daring to look upon her Queen before instructed to.

"I shall tend to you in a moment," Sealiah said. "And rise. Submission becomes most young girls . . . but not you."

The Queen of Poppies had dressed to kill today. A sheath of gossamer metal clung to her curves—liquid dark-matter silver that had been in existence before the mortal Earth had been dust gathering in void.

Jezebel's gaze settled on the emerald that sat in the delicate V of Sealiah's collarbone. This stone was the personal symbol of Sealiah's power. It pulsed, daring any who desired it to try to rip it from her.

Jezebel had a sliver of that stone within her left palm—a gift and living link to her Queen.

Her fingers rolled into a fist. How she would love to taste more.

She averted her eyes from this obvious temptation, however, and her gaze landed upon the curved daggers, Exarp and Omebb, strapped to Sealiah's thighs . . . as well as the broken Sword of Dread, Saliceran, sheathed on her hip.

That terrible blade was said to have been broken as it struck the Immovable One in the Great War with

Heaven. It had killed thousands of mortals and Immortals. The metal wept venom equal to the rage of the one who wielded it.

Jezebel then turned her attentions to the map table. It was a model of the Poppy Lands from the Valley of the Shadow of Death across the Dusk End of Rainbow to Venom-Tangle Thicket. Miniature infantry and fungus bat squadrons, Lancers of the Wild Rose, and Longbow of the Order of Whispering Death guarded key strategic locations . . . waiting for the enemy to make its move.

Bumblebees flew from open windows and landed upon the table. Covered in pollen and sticky with nectar, they waddled, buzzing among the unit markers and pushing them to their latest positions.

Sealiah plucked up one black-and-amber insect, its stinger half the length of its squirming body. "Tell the Lancers to pull back to the Western Ridge. Bury antipersonnel mines as they go." She then blew on the creature, and it took to the air.

"Now," Sealiah said, and finally turned to Jezebel, "how was school?"

Her Queen was, as always, breathtaking: bronze skin, her hair gleaming copper and streaked with platinum, and eyes that knew the depths of seduction and addiction.

Jezebel had to resist the urge to fall down in worship. "I passed entrance and placement exams without incident, my Queen."

The entrance to the Paxington Institute had been obvious to her Infernal senses. And between the answers provided for her, as well as weeks of intensive study from tutors, Jezebel had earned a B+ on the written exam, of which she was extremely proud.

Her former incarnation, Julie Marks—when she bothered to go to high school at all—had scraped by with Cs.

"Of course you passed." Sealiah arched one delicate eyebrow. "Or you would dare not show your face here."

Jezebel felt her cheeks heat, and she carefully averted her eyes so her Queen did not see the hate within.

"Tell me about the twins," Sealiah ordered.

On a side table, the Queen unrolled the circular mat for a game of Towers, a game that to Jezebel seemed part checkers, part chess, and had a long list of rules that seemed improvised half the time.

"They passed their tests, too. We are on the same team: Scarab." Jezebel continued with a narration of their first day, explaining the composition of their team (including a report on Robert Farmington, who surely worked for the League), their tour of the Paxington campus, and the Ludus Magnus.

She told Sealiah how Fiona and Eliot reacted to it all. How they were so naïve about everything. It was pathetic.

"You think your Eliot Post is weak, then?"

"No, my Queen. There is something still to the boy. I can feel it growing within him. Something that . . ."

Jezebel couldn't find the words. She wasn't sure how she felt about him . . . something no doubt left over from her weaker, mortal self.

"You are drawn to the boy?" Sealiah narrowed her eyes at Jezebel as she searched her heart. "Beyond his mere power?"

Jezebel opened her mouth to deny any attraction.

But that would be a lie. One her Queen would instantly detect. Such simple deceptions were the greatest insult one Infernal could give to another.

So she said nothing.

Sealiah inspected her nails: bloodred and pointed. She then set a handful of white cubes upon the Towers game mat. "Does he suspect who you were?"

"He may." Jezebel fidgeted. "He looks at me—I mean, like all the boys, of course. But, I think he sees a shadow of . . . she who I was." Jezebel couldn't speak her former name aloud. She loathed the weak creature she had been. "It shall not be a problem. It will be child's play to deflect his questions."

Sealiah stroked Jezebel's cheek with one fingernail, cutting the flesh. The sensation sent shivers through Jezebel. "You will tell him the truth if he asks," Sealiah said. "All of it. Even, and *especially,* about Julie Marks."

Jezebel inhaled and took an involuntary step back.

"I don't understand," she said. "I thought I was to get close to the twins. Help them so they would be sympathetic to our cause. Wasn't I going to be friends with Fiona? With Eliot? How will the truth help that?"

Jezebel realized too late that withdrawal from her Queen's presence, questioning her orders—either could be reason to be annihilated.

Sealiah, however, merely smiled and tilted her head. "These are still our goals, my pet. But Eliot is far more Infernal than any yet suspect. I have reports of his music quelling the borders of the disputed Blasted Lands."

Eliot had been to Hell? Jezebel wanted to ask how and when and what he had played.

For a terrible moment, she was Julie Marks again, yearning to hear *her* song once more. Her heart filled with hope and love and light.

She quickly snuffed those weaknesses before Sealiah saw them—and ripped them from her chest.

Still . . . she didn't understand.

Sealiah must have seen the confusion on her face, because she said, "If the boy continues to develop his stronger, Infernal nature, then he will certainly be able to do what any young lord of Hell can: sort lies from truth."

Jezebel wrestled with her Queen's command to tell the truth. Deception had been the entire basis of her relationship with Eliot. He had fallen for sweet, innocent, and vulnerable Julie Marks, the new manager at Ringo's Pizza—not runaway, died-of-a-heroin-overdose Julie Marks from the alleyways of Atlanta, not Julie Marks who had made a deal for her life and soul in exchange for seducing him into damnation everlasting.

"Shhh," Sealiah said, "quiet your thoughts." She looked down upon her, her features a mix of pity and disgust. "Since you have yet to be trained on the higher arts of trickery, our young Eliot will sense any attempt to hide the truth—so do not. It would backfire and further alienate you from him."

"I shall do as you say, my Queen," Jezebel said. "But . . . won't he hate me?"

"Oh, my precious dear—of course he will. How much you have yet to learn of men."

Sealiah drew Jezebel closer and slipped her arms about her shoulder. This felt wonderfully warm and comforting and yet terribly dangerous at the same time.

"Eliot *will* hate you, at first. But you will then have the boy's interest . . . which, when mixed with his good intentions and budding manly concerns, will curdle into love."

Jezebel understood. She didn't like her part in it, but she nonetheless appreciated the cleverness of the ploy—

both dreaming of *and* dreading what would happen to her and Eliot when it came to fruition.

"Then," Sealiah said, glancing at her game of Towers, "we will have him."

16

❧

BREAKFAST SPECIAL

Eliot ran along the sidewalk. Fiona raced him to the spot on the granite wall where the entrance to Paxington hid in plain sight.

He'd gotten a few paces ahead of her because she had to dodge a flower cart parked on the sidewalk (and she was too prissy to run around it on the street—even a few feet).

He stopped at the wall, touched it, and panted.

She shrugged as if to say, *Whatever—I let you,* but couldn't speak because she was breathing too heavily.

Eliot knew they wouldn't be late today—absolutely not.

He'd learned how to set the alarm on his new phone and gotten up extra early. He hadn't wanted to take any chances, though, so he and Fiona raced all the way from the breakfast table down through Pacific Heights, onto Lombard Street to here.

Eliot opened his phone, double-checking that they had plenty of time to make it to class. They did.

He found the crack in the wall, focused on it, and

this time it was easy to slip around the corner that shouldn't exist.

It still felt weird.

Fiona came in right behind him.

The alley to Paxington was shaded, and the ivy-covered walls cooled the already chilly air. Café Eridanus was full, the outdoor tables taken by older students eating pastries and drinking lattes before school started.

Eliot paused and inhaled scents wafting from the café: freshly ground coffee and steamed milk, a slightly charred citrus odor from flaming crêpes suzettes, melting butter, bacon, and sourdough bread just out of the oven.

"Come on," Fiona said, and moved toward the gate.

Eliot's stomach complained, and he lingered. He would die if he had to sit through an entire lecture, or at the very least, he wouldn't be able to hear Miss Westin speaking over his grumbling digestive tract.

"Just a sec," he said. "I'll grab a bite—"

Eliot's mind halted mid-thought. Even his stomach stopped rumbling.

His father sat at one of the outdoor café tables under the sky blue canopy. Three older Paxington boys stood around him, so Eliot hadn't seen him at first.

The plates and coffee cups at his table had been shoved aside. Louis moved his hands over the table-cloth, shuffling three cards.

"Don't take your eyes off it this time," Louis told the boys. "Not for an instant!"

Eliot edged closer. Fiona was right behind him.

Louis's cards were facedown on the table, and each creased down the center so they could be easily manip-ulated. One was dog-eared. Another had a water spot in the center.

Eliot felt something off . . . and understood Louis was trying to fool the boys by making the shuffling look so simple and the cards so easy to identify.

"Now," Louis asked the boys. "Where is the Queen of Spades?"

"That one." A boy pointed to the center card.

Another told him, "No, it's the one on the right."

Louis smiled. "Are you *sure?*"

He looked up as he said this, and caught Eliot's eyes. Something passed between them, a slight tilt of the head, recognition, and an invitation to watch and learn.

"I'm sure," the boy said, "the center card. Flip it already and pay up."

Louis obliged. The card was the three of hearts.

"I'm sorry," Louis said, genuinely sounding sad. "You'll get it next time, I'm sure." He scooped their money off the table.

The boys asked for one more game, but Louis said no. "I have other customers this morning." He gestured at Eliot and Fiona.

The three boys left, muttering and arguing over how they had lost track of the queen.

Eliot and Fiona moved to the table.

"You came here to see us, didn't you?" Eliot asked.

"Of course, my boy." Louis clasped him warmly by the shoulder. "You look dashing in that uniform, by the way. The girls shall swoon."

Eliot felt instantly two feet taller.

Louis turned to Fiona. "And you, my dearest Fiona, you look . . ." He gesticulated with his hands, but couldn't find the right words as he looked her over. "So nice."

Fiona crossed her arms over her chest. "You're not supposed to be here."

"True," Louis said. "I am often not where I am supposed to be. And your mother *has* promised to kill me if I ever came near you again." He shrugged. "But she does not know of this meeting, so the point is moot." He stood, pulled out a chair, and gallantly offered it to Fiona.

Fiona remained standing and glared at him.

Louis was unfazed by this. He looked for the waiter, saying, "Let us not dwell on the ugly past and all these wretched parental custody issues, shall we? Let us just forgive one another, order breakfast, and chat. There's so much lost time to make up for."

"Forgive each other?" Fiona said. "What have *we* done that needs *your* forgiveness?"

Louis raised a finger. "Tut-tut. I won't hear of it. All is forgotten and pardoned."

Eliot sat.

Sure, he was still mad at Louis for using them as bait to lure Beelzebub into a trap (a trap, by the way, that hadn't worked). Only by the narrowest of scrapes had they not been killed. And sure, Louis was an Infernal, the Prince of Darkness, and perhaps evil incarnate. But he was their only relation who had ever given them straight answers. Something in very short supply these days.

Besides, Eliot was hungry.

A waiter came and took out a notepad.

"Shall it be two or three specials?" Louis asked Fiona.

She toyed with the rubber band on her wrist, and then reluctantly settled into the chair.

"Ten minutes," she told Eliot. "No more. If we're late again for class . . ."

"Yes," Louis purred, "Miss Westin once had a guillotine for her tardy students." He looked utterly serious and he made a chopping motion onto the table. "Three specials," he told the waiter. "Make it a rush."

"Oui, Monsieur Piper."

Eliot studied his father. He looked so different from the dirty homeless person he'd been just a few months ago . . . and definitely different from the bat-winged fallen-angel woodcuts he'd seen in *Paradise Lost* (part of last night's reading assignment). Louis wore black slacks and a black silk dress shirt undone to his sternum (with buttons that looked like real diamonds). Eliot thought this might be what a stage magician would look like.

But it was Louis's face that fascinated Eliot most. His eyes sparkled as if he had just been laughing; his nose was crooked and hooked at the end; his thin mustache and goatee were immaculately trimmed and pointed; and his silver-streaked hair had been pulled back. It gave him an air of casual grace, elegance, and above all else . . . mischief.

"What do you want?" Fiona asked their father.

"What I want?" Louis got a faraway look in his eyes and stroked his chin. "I want my family to be whole and happy. I want you two to graduate from Paxington *maxima cum laude,* bar none, *merito puro*! I want to sail a galleon of solid gold upon a lake of jewels in my treasure kingdom the size of Nevada! I want the love of a beautiful woman. All women! I want the respect and adulation of billions. I want the world to be my pearl-stuffed oyster!"

Louis made eye contact with the waiter. "Although," he said with a sigh, "I'd settle for a cup of this establishment's wonderful Turkish coffee. What about you, darling daughter?"

"I want you to stop calling me that," she said.

"I want answers," Eliot chimed in before his sister worked up a head of steam.

Louis brightened and turned to him. "And so you shall have them, my boy. Ask! Anything. I shall be your unbiased oracle."

The waiter brought coffee and orange juice and a basket of steaming blueberry muffins drizzled with butter.

Eliot tore into a muffin, drank half a glass of juice, and then said, "Uncle Kino drove us to the Gates of Perdition. To show us where Infernals come from. Was it really Hell? Is that where you live?"

Louis considered for a moment, and slipped four sugar cubes into his coffee. "He showed you . . . yes, but only the absolutely most wretched part. It's like driving through the worst sections of Detroit and being told that is America. Why, you'd miss out entirely on Disneyland and Las Vegas."

"Please," Fiona scoffed. "Are you saying there are *nice* parts of Hell?"

"There are forests, jungles, and cities filled with exotic delights," Louis said. "There are circuses, meadows of flowers, castles filled with lords and ladies—realms beyond imagination."

Eliot leaned forward.

He half hoped Louis would invite him to see for himself. He'd never take him up on such an offer, not after they'd seen what lay beyond the gate in the Borderlands . . . but still, it'd be wonderful to learn a little bit more about his father's side of the family.

And just for a moment, Eliot considered the possibility of life beyond his mother's influence. He and Louis could be adventurers, pirates on the high seas, travelers and explorers.

Fiona, however, looked unconvinced.

"None of that matters to us," she told Louis. "We're in the League now." She kicked Eliot under the table. "Both of us. I'm in the Order of the Celestial Rose. And Eliot is an Immortal hero."

"Congratulations," Louis said without enthusiasm.

Breakfast arrived: plates with a stack of crêpes drenched with brandied sauce, a side of sizzling bacon, and steaming fresh croissants. The waiter set the bill next to Louis's plate . . . which Louis ignored.

Eliot tasted the bacon. It was crisp and salty and wonderful. But something stopped him from enjoying it: Fiona's assertion that they were in the League. Around a mouthful, he said to her, "Okay—so we're part of the League of Immortals . . . but why does that mean we're *not* part of the other family? That makes no sense from a biological point of view."

Fiona glared at him, but for the moment, she had no answer.

It occurred to Eliot that he was breaking a rule by talking of the League in public. Then again, no one here seemed to be listening. Nor could this alley outside Paxington truly be considered a public place.

Or was it just easier for Eliot to break rules when his father was near? Louis had once told him: Everything was made to be broken, especially rules.

Right now, Eliot didn't care; he just wanted answers.

"You are both," Louis told them. "Immortal *and* Infernal."

"That's not what the League's decided," Fiona said.

"I'm afraid the facts speak louder. You, my darling daughter—" Louis stopped, remembering that Fiona didn't like him calling her that. "You killed Beelzebub."

Fiona paled.

Eliot lost his appetite as well when he remembered how she had severed Beelzebub's head.

"There's a neutrality treaty between the League and us," Louis said, "which prevents any such physical interventions."

"But it was self-defense," Eliot said.

"Of course it was," Louis replied. "The reason is irrelevant. My point is that you must *be* an Infernal to *kill* another Infernal. And you must be an Immortal to be legally accepted into the League of Immortals. These are immutable facts with a single conclusion. . . ."

"That we're both?" Eliot tentatively offered.

A faint smile spread across Louis's face.

"So what?" Fiona said. "We decided to stick with the League. It's our choice."

"And an admirable choice it is," Louis replied. "But I'm afraid there are those who will not care what you have chosen. Some think you are the means to unravel our neutrality treaty. Some believe that one day you will lead one side to war against the other."

War? Louis had to be joking.

But for once, he looked absolutely serious.

"We would never do such a thing," Eliot whispered.

"Never? Really?" Louis asked. "Not even in self-defense? Could you envision some unscrupulous character manipulating you into a situation where conflict might be inevitable?"

Fiona was quiet, probably reliving that moment in the alley when she had decapitated the Lord of All That Flies.

Eliot wanted to say that he'd never kill anything or anybody . . . but then he remembered that to save Fiona, he had summoned a fog filled with the wandering dead. It was a mistake the first time, but he'd known what he was doing the second time, and he'd still done it. He *had* killed. And it'd been his choice.

Eliot knew he would do it again if Fiona's life were at stake.

He pushed his plate away, no longer hungry.

"So what do we do?" Eliot asked.

"What you think is right," Louis told him, leaning closer. "You two are smarter and stronger than anyone in the families knows. You would do best not to listen to deceitful characters who would try to influence you. Besides, of course, your father."

When Louis turned to Fiona, his expression sobered, and he searched for the right words, finally saying, "Within you burns the fury of all the Hells, unquenchable and unstoppable . . . and yet you somehow manage to rein in that power. Truly impressive, my daughter."

"Thank you," Fiona said. "I think."

He turned to Eliot. "And you, my son, have a talent the likes of which the world has never before seen. Not even my humble abilities come close. When you play, the universe holds its breath . . . and listens."

Eliot wanted to say so much more, ask Louis so many things, but it felt as if he'd just swallowed too much information, and it stuck in his windpipe.

Louis stood. "You two are going to be late if we sit all day chitchatting like sparrows over crumbs." He dug into his pockets. "Before I depart, I wanted to give you some trinkets I had lying about."

He tossed one of the playing cards to Eliot.

It fluttered, and to Eliot's utter astonishment, he snatched it out of the air with nimble fingers.

The card was the Queen of Spades, but not a normal one. This queen held a sword like a suicide king—stuck through the side of her head. Most intriguing, though, there were tiny lines and dots scribbled upon it.

Notes. Musical notes.

"'The March of the Suicide Queen,'" Louis told him. "It's an old song that you may find useful."

Eliot touched the notes, and heard them whisper their tune to him.

He tucked the card into his pocket for a closer look later. He wanted to thank Louis, but then remembered that the other songs he'd gotten from his father had led to death and destruction.

He kept his mouth shut and simply nodded.

"And for you, Fiona . . ." Louis smoothed a silver bracelet over the tablecloth. Its slender twisted links reminded Eliot of a snake. "This was made from the last bit of metal that fell from the sky millennia ago. Archon iron."[20]

Fiona picked up the bracelet and examined it. "I don't know what to say. Thank you!" She frowned. "Is it *supposed* to be rusty?"

"The price of antiquity, I am afraid," Louis assured her.

Their father bowed, clasped Eliot's shoulder once more, and gently patted Fiona's hand. "We will meet again soon, I hope. Now you must pardon your poor misremembering father, but he has other business to attend to."

And with that, Louis plucked up his jacket, strode

---

20. Archon iron. A mythohistorical metal said to have fallen from Heaven—literally fallout from the war between God and his rebellious angels, preceding their fall from grace. The metal was an ingredient in the manufacture of the chain binding the wolf Fenrir (prior to its release during Ragnarök). See also Volume 11, the *Post Family Mythology*, for more on this wondrous and terrible element wielded by Fiona Post during the Last Judgment War, which ended the Fifth Age. *Gods of the First and Twenty-first Century, Volume 4, Core Myths (Part 1).* Zypheron Press Ltd., Eighth Edition.

out of the café, turned onto the main street, and was gone.

Fiona gazed at the chain. "We need to think about what he said . . . everything."

"So maybe Louis isn't all bad?" Eliot asked her.

She looped the bracelet around her wrist and did the clasp. "Maybe," Fiona said.

Was it possible this was the beginning of a real relationship with their father? So what if he was an Infernal? Maybe even a man who was supposed to be living, breathing evil could still care for his son.

Eliot and Fiona got up to leave. They miraculously still had plenty of time to get to class.

As they started to go, however, the waiter followed them, clearing his throat. In his hand was the bill that had been left untouched on the table.

Fiona's face darkened, and Eliot took back all the nice things he had thought about Louis.

He'd stiffed them for breakfast.

17

୧

FRIENDS AND ENEMIES

Fiona was mortified. Nothing like this ever happened in homeschooling. She'd never had to undress in front of other people.

She was grateful she hadn't worn her gym shorts and T-shirt *under* her school uniform. That's how she thought it might work. She'd tried it at home, but the extra layers only added to the wrinkled appearance of her jacket and skirt.

The Paxington girls' locker room had only the illusion of privacy. There were rows of benches and lockers so you couldn't see *everyone* at the same time. But still, within the range of a casual glance, dozens of girls laughed and chatted as they stripped out of their uniforms like this was the most ordinary thing in the world.

Fiona didn't think she could blush any harder as she struggled with the buttons on her shirt.

Maybe it was a lifetime of eating Cee's home cooking, maybe it was her severed appetite, but she felt so skinny, so . . . unendowed, compared with the other girls.

Plus all these other girls had perfect manes of hair. Fiona's hair (thanks to the foggy morning) was all frizz.

Not to mention they all wore makeup. They had purses bulging with lipstick and powders, liners and every brush imaginable.

Fiona had used Cee's homemade soap, which efficiently removed dirt (and your first layer of skin), but didn't really enhance anyone's beauty.

Fortunately no one noticed her.

She looked at her feet and focused on slipping out of her skirt and into her gym shorts as fast as she could.

Fiona would have done it with her eyes closed if she wasn't afraid she might have done something dorky like put them on backward.

She'd never look like these girls. They'd had fifteen years to perfect their looks. They had every modern product and advantage.

She'd just have to be happy with who she was and

how she looked . . . though that was easier said than done. Who was she, really? Immortal? A goddess-in-training with the League of Immortals? Or an Infernal? The daughter of the Prince of Darkness?

Both?

But then why did she still look like Fiona Post, shut-in, social and beauty moron?

Louis showing up this morning had thrown her off. She hadn't expected to feel anything for him . . . or if she had, she expected it would have been contempt. He still sounded half crazy, but there was something else there: a spark of wit and intelligence.

He was her father, and she *wanted* to feel a bond with him. She wanted to have something approaching a normal relationship . . . at least with one of her parents. Was that too much to ask?

Jezebel sauntered into the locker room. The girls fell silent.

The Infernal stepped up to the locker next to Fiona's, opened it, and removed her jacket.

Fiona started to say hi, but Jezebel (although she had to see her; she was standing right there) acted like she was completely alone in the locker room.

Jezebel shrugged out of her top and bra.

Fiona quickly turned away.

But not before she caught a glimpse of Jezebel's snow-white porcelain skin, ample curves, and taut stomach. Like pictures Fiona had seen recently in her mythology books—that's how goddesses were *supposed* to look. Or demons.

A girl approached Jezebel and cleared her throat.

Jezebel ignored her.

The girl was tall, tan, blond, and athletic. Fiona remembered her from team selection. She was on White Knight.

"Hey." The girl confidently leaned on a nearby locker. "I'm Tamara. A bunch of us were going to grab coffee after class today. You want to hang out?"

"I don't care who you are," Jezebel told her. "What makes you think that I have need for coffee . . . or the company of mortals?"

Tamara's features bunched together in outrage. "Why, you little bit—!"

Jezebel turned.

The air was charged with tension. The hair on the back of Fiona's neck prickled.

Jezebel's shadow crossed Tamara, darkening her face.

But that was wrong. Fiona checked her own shadow—yes, the overhead lights cast several weak shadows in various directions. Jezebel's shadow somehow defied the optics of the situation, and had collected into a single slice of dark.

Whatever Tamara was going to say, she didn't. The breath seemed to have evaporated from her lungs.

"You will find that I have no tolerance for trifling," Jezebel said. "Decide now if you wish to live."

Tamara took two steps back. "Never mind," she whispered.

Jezebel's shadow returned to normal.

Fiona exhaled.

Tamara managed to regain a bit of her composure, although her healthy tan seemed to have drained away. "Whatever . . ." She walked off—banging her shin on a bench.

Jezebel gave a stifled laugh, then opened her locker and primped the curls of her hair (although it didn't need it), and then continued ignoring the rest of the world.

Fiona made a mental note: *Do not make small talk with an Infernal.*

She smelled mint and turned. Sarah Covington stood next to her. Sarah's red hair had been pulled back and tucked up under a white baseball cap. "Don't worry about that," Sarah said conspiratorially. "Tamara's just sussing out the pecking order."

Sarah offered Fiona a stick of gum, which she accepted to be polite, but didn't unwrap.

"I'm dying to know about the girl who saved my cousin," Sarah said. "No one is *supposed* to come back from the Valley of the New Year. You said your family name was . . ."

"Post," Fiona said, nervous, as if this were the answer to a pop quiz.

"As in 'as dumb as'?" Sarah smiled and laughed. "I'm just jesting, my dear. You must take care not to take any of that nonsense from the other girls, or they'll walk all over you for the next four years."

Fiona didn't like being called dumb—even as a joke. Especially as a joke.

Despite Sarah Covington's outward kindness, Fiona didn't think that's what her teammate had in mind by coming over here and chatting. Her instincts told her this was another test. Not an official Paxington-sanctioned pencil-and-paper test. One more important.

Fiona straightened. "The last person who tried to 'walk all over' me and Eliot . . . didn't do *any* walking afterward."

Fiona had to soothe the anger coiled within her like a sleeping dragon, knowing how easily it could be aroused . . . knowing, too, that despite her dorky appearance, she *was* special . . . powerful . . . and if she had to be, dangerous, too.

The smile on Sarah's freckled face faded. "Yes, I can indeed see a bit of the spark that got you and my cousin out of Purgatory." She looked as if she had more to say to Fiona, but her gaze then caught something intriguing across the locker room. "Excuse me. There's a bit of unfinished business to take care of."

Fiona watched Sarah flounce off.

Jezebel glanced at Fiona—with neither approval nor disdain—which Fiona guessed was what passed for a friendly gesture in Infernal circles.

Sarah moved to where Amanda Lane was awkwardly trying to tuck her T-shirt (which was three sizes too big) into her baggy shorts.

Fiona hadn't seen Amanda when she came in. She had mastered social invisibility, and Fiona understood why. If no one ever saw you, you didn't have to struggle to find the right words, and then stumble and stutter them out in the unlikely case someone actually spoke to you.

She knew all this because that's just the silent subspecies of nerd she had been only a few months ago.

In many ways, she still was, and everything she was trying to be—poised, confident, and likable—was just an act.

"I don't recall inviting *you* to Team Scarab," Sarah told Amanda so sweetly that she could have been talking about the weather.

"I didn't . . . ," Amanda started. She swiped her straggly hair out of her face, but it fell immediately back. She looked at the ground. "I mean, my name was on the roster posted outside."

"Then that's a mistake," Sarah said, jabbing at her for emphasis. "You need to find another team. And quickly, so we can find a suitable replacement."

"But, I thought . . ." Amanda's voice faded to nothing.

"You said you were sponsored to Paxington by the League?" Sarah asked. "Of Immortals? Truly? Not the League of Losers? Or is this one of the gods' practical jokes?" Sarah grabbed a handful of Amanda's T-shirt, yanked it out of her shorts—then shoved her. "Or are you just a liar?"

Amanda banged into her locker and winced.

Fiona took an involuntary step closer. Her first instinct was to rush over there and stop this.

But she halted. Part of her wanted to know why Amanda was here, too. She knew Amanda wouldn't lie about the League sponsorship. Why had they sent her here?

Sarah pressed on, however, before Fiona could act. She grasped Amanda by her arm and shoved her into the showers.

The other girls watched, some laughed, but most just kept doing what they were doing.

"No," Amanda whimpered. She didn't even look up, her eyes firmly glued to her feet, unwilling—or maybe unable—to stand up for herself.

Amanda stumbled onto the tiled stalls. "Please don't," she whispered to Sarah.

"'Please'?" Sarah said, mocking her. "Please help you get clean? Help you wash that rat's nest hair? Why, certainly."

Sarah twisted on a cold water spigot. A shower nozzle sputtered and shot forth streams of water.

It hit Amanda, and she yelped, then jumped out of the way.

Sarah tapped the pipe. All the cold water spigots turned by themselves. Icy water rained and filled the entire shower section of the locker room.

Amanda backed into the corner, but still got drenched.

"St-st-stop it," Amanda sobbed. "Please."

Fiona had watched enough. Someone had to stand up for Amanda. And someone had to take that horrid Sarah Covington down a few notches.

She marched over to them. "Turn it off," Fiona told Sarah.

Sarah looked around the gym, pursed her lips, and appeared for a split second as uneasy with this cruel prank as Fiona . . . but then she shook her head.

Fiona reached for the water faucet—Sarah stepped in front of her.

Fiona wanted to punch Sarah right in her petite button nose, freckles and all.

But she checked the impulse as she remembered how she had fought Beelzebub. She'd hit and been hit with enough force to smash concrete. If she hit Sarah *that* hard, the girl might not survive.

And as tempting as that was, at this particular moment, Fiona knew violence was wrong.

So instead she reached for the main pipe, her fingers slipped over the beads of condensation on the metal, and she closed her hand—crushing the steel as if it were an empty aluminum can.

The water in the pipe squeaked and squealed and stuttered to a stop.

Louis had told her: "*Within you burns the fury of all the Hells, unquenchable and unstoppable . . . and yet you somehow manage to rein in that power.*"

. . . Maybe not *entirely* reined in at this moment.

Fiona released the mashed pipe and turned to Sarah. Her hand slowly clenched into a fist in front of Sarah's face. "She's on our team," Fiona told her. "But if you don't like it—*you* don't have to be."

Sarah glanced at the crushed pipe, seemingly unimpressed, then looked at Fiona's fist. Her eyes narrowed a tad. She didn't look frightened, but nonetheless she snorted and backed off a step, then returned to her locker.

"'Just sussing out the pecking order,'" Fiona muttered after her.

Fiona might never be Sarah's social equal at Paxington—but if she could help it, she wasn't going to be bullied or let her bully anyone else.

Fiona went to Amanda.

The girl stood shivering in the corner, wet hair plastered over her face. She tried to control her sobs, but they still came out in little gasps.

Fiona was about to offer her hand to the girl . . . but then thought better of it. Probably not the smartest thing to do after she had just crushed the pipe in front of her.

For a moment she wondered if Sarah hadn't been right in one sense: Amanda didn't belong here. She was going to get hurt. Or worse.

Why had the League sent her here anyway?

"It's going to be okay," Fiona said, amazingly sounding like she meant this.

"Th-th-thanks." The word shuddered out of Amanda's body.

"Let's get you toweled off," Fiona suggested. "I have an extra set of gym clothes you can borrow."

Amanda nodded and skittered out of the showers.

Fiona considered what she had done by saving Amanda: she'd have to watch out not only for herself and her brother—but now a third clueless person as well. That was going to be trouble.

These thoughts came skidding to a halt, however.

The water at Fiona's feet steamed.

It wasn't cold the way it should have been. It bubbled, boiling hot.

18

&

THE UNPREPARED TEST

Eliot had changed into his shorts and gym T-shirt (which had a nifty gold scarab embroidered on the right breast) and now stood on the field before the six-story-high obstacle course in the Ludus Magnus coliseum.

If there'd ever been a jungle gym event in the Olympics, *this* would have been it.

There were simple things like stairs, slides, and monkey bars—most of which were fifty feet high, though. There were less childlike things: rope bridges, balance beams, and zip lines. Then there were the things that looked dangerous: barbed wire mazes, and platforms held by single poles that swayed (even in no wind).

Eliot took a deep breath. He wasn't afraid of heights . . . but even unafraid, you'd have to be nuts to climb this thing.

He'd had a week to prepare for his first gym class, a week he had spent with his nose stuck in books on myths, gods, and demons. He'd learned tons, but he should have been jogging, or doing push-ups or something to get ready for this.

One good fall and a busted neck . . . and all that reading would be moot.

Next to him, Jeremy Covington droned on to Mitch Stephenson about classic winning strategies on the Ludus Magnus course.

Mitch caught Eliot's uneasy look and, with a flick of his head, invited him to join them.

Eliot waved back but didn't approach.

In the last week, Jeremy had barely said five words to him. The Scotsman was a bully. He'd been in three fights—won them all with kicks to the groin and thumb jabs to the eyes. Eliot was also pretty sure he smelled whiskey on his breath yesterday, too.

Mitch, on the other hand, got along with everyone. He always said hi, had something cool to say, paid attention in class—he'd even protected poor clueless Amanda from getting hassled. But Mitch also kept everyone at arm's length, like he used his friendliness as an invisible shield.

Standing to Eliot's left were four boys. Eliot had seen them on campus, but didn't know them.

On these boys' black shirts was a different symbol: a white sword crossed over a white lance. They were Team White Knight.

Eliot had read that White Knights were supposed to be the good guys. The polite thing to do would have been to introduce himself . . . but from the boys' cold assessing looks, he didn't think they were here to rescue any damsels or do good deeds.

They whispered and nodded at the jungle gym— from the snippets Eliot overheard, coming up with a strategy to beat Team Scarab.

Eliot kept his distance. He wanted to be friends with everyone, but something told him that being friends might get in the way of winning.

It seemed Paxington had been engineered to promote a philosophy of "win at any cost" with its duels, academic bell curve, gym class, and social pecking order. But Eliot didn't want to win if so many others had to lose.

Robert came out of the boys' locker room and jogged over to Eliot. "Almost didn't get here today," he said. "Slept in."

He had a faded bruise around one eye, like he'd been in a fight recently. His T-shirt was taut and flexed with muscle. He must be working out.

"I've been trying to catch you all week," Eliot said, "but you're gone as soon as the class bell rings."

"Just studying," he said without meeting Eliot's gaze. "That reading stuff comes easy for you . . . not so much for a guy like me."

All this was true, but it felt a bit off, like Robert had left out one important fact.

Eliot guessed what it was. "Are you avoiding Fiona on purpose?"

Robert took a big breath and sighed. "Probably," he said. "Some folks in the League think I got off too light for breaking their rules. I could get Fiona in trouble just being seen with her."

Eliot had figured as much. He wanted to have a long talk with Robert. Partially because he thought of him as a friend. Partially because Eliot needed someone to talk to . . . someone who wasn't getting more and more concerned with how they looked, staying locked inside the bathroom every morning. It was like Fiona thought her hair was more important than school.

Before he could say more to Robert, however, four girls marched onto the field. They stood with the White Knight boys and eyed Eliot and Robert with a mix of curiosity and contempt. The White Knight boys spoke to the girls, pointing at the gym structure.

Jezebel then emerged from the girls' locker room, followed a moment later by Sarah Covington.

"We'll talk," Robert said, "but later. Catch me after gym today, okay?"

Eliot nodded.

"Does the Infernal . . . ," Robert whispered. "I know this sounds nuts, but she looks like that girl you hung out with this summer. What was her name?"

"Julie Marks."

Eliot had thought it was just him, but she really did look like Julie. Uncurl her hair, add a little color to the dead white skin, and she could have been Julie's twin.

But believing that was wishful thinking. Julie had been mortal; the only extraordinary thing about her was that she had liked Eliot. She even kissed him, before she'd left Del Sombra for Hollywood. Remembering made Eliot feel wonderful and miserable all at the same time.

Sarah Covington waved Eliot and Robert over to where the girls, Jeremy, and Mitch now stood.

Eliot grabbed his pack off the grass and they joined his teammates.

"Where's Fiona and Amanda?" Eliot asked.

"There was a wee issue," Sarah told him, and tucked a strand of red hair into her cap. "A girl thing. They'll be out in a jiffy."

Jeremy cleared his throat. "We need to be thinking up a strategy," he told them. "First, we pick the Team Captain."

"You?" Robert snorted.

"Who else?" Jeremy said. "I've studied freshman gym extensively. I know all the tactics."

The thought of taking orders from Jeremy made Eliot's skin crawl. "Seems simple to me," Eliot countered. "Get to your flag before the others do."

Sarah looked at Eliot like he was a bug. "You think it's so simple? I can't wait to see how you do up there."

Eliot matched her stare. "Sure, it's going to be harder than that. But what about Robert or Mitch . . . or

Jezebel? It'd be nice to have someone leading us who—I don't know—knows something about modern technology, like cell phones, for instance?"

Jeremy's smile vanished.

"What do cell phones have to do with gym?" Mitch asked.

"Field communications," Robert said, nodding. "We can get a conference call going. We should get headsets, too."

"Perhaps," Jezebel told Eliot, "you should be Team Captain."

She said this without inflection. Eliot wasn't sure if it was a joke. Her jade green eyes were not like Julie's clear blue eyes at all . . . yet they had the same sparkle.

"Please m'lady," Jeremy said. "We need someone with experience in these matters. Someone maybe who has struck another in anger before? . . . In case such a far-fetched possibility occurs."

"So fighting's the goal?" Eliot spat back. "Or getting to our flag and winning?"

If Jeremy wanted his résumé on fighting, he could tell him about the ten thousand rats he and Fiona had faced in the sewers, or Perry Millhouse, or an entire air force base, or the Infernal Lord of All That Flies.

Fiona and Amanda stepped out of the girls' locker room, and seeing those two halted Eliot's thoughts.

Amanda wore a stunned expression. Her hair was wet as if she'd just taken a shower. But *before* gym class?

Eliot caught Fiona's eyes and she gave a shake of her head. Something had happened, but she couldn't tell him—not now.

He met Fiona halfway and said, "We're trying to figure out a strategy. Jeremy wants to pick a Captain first. It's so stupid."

"*He's* so stupid," Fiona said. She turned to Amanda. "Can you do this? Maybe you better sit it out."

"No." A spark of life returned to Amanda's dark eyes. "I'm okay."

Fiona stalked over to the rest of their team. She was mad, at whom Eliot didn't know, but he felt the anger coming off his sister in waves.

"Ah, Fiona, me darling," Jeremy said, "we be ready to vote for a Captain. I know I can count on your support."

"You don't have a Team Captain yet?" one of the girls from White Knight said. She was tall, tan, and stood with her hands on her hips—and she had obviously been eavesdropping. "What a bunch of losers."

"Mind your own business, Tamara," Sarah told her. "We'll see who'll be losing soon enough."

"What do you expect?" one of the White Knight boys with a shaven head remarked. "They have an Infernal on their team. They've got to be disorganized."

Jezebel turned to see who had said this, but her expression didn't change, nor did she say a thing.

Somehow this scared Eliot more than if she had threatened him with hellfire.

"Hey!" Robert yelled back. "You're going to sound pretty funny with a mouthful of fist, buddy."

"Bring it," the boy said, taking a step forward.

Mitch set a hand on Robert's arm. "Save it for class," he advised.

The air stilled and Eliot felt something. *Felt,* however, wasn't quiet right, because this was just an itch below his threshold of conscious detection . . . a whispered warning that danger was near.

He, Fiona, and Jezebel turned.

A man walked onto the field. He held a clipboard and stopwatch. He wore black sweats with the Paxington crest. He moved with strength, confidence, and grace. He was darkly tanned and trim and very old. Deep laugh lines and wrinkles made a spiderweb of his face. His hair was white, thick, and gathered into a long tail.

Eliot felt the weight of the Ages on this old man. As if he'd seen everything and that nothing Eliot could do would ever impress him.

"I am Mr. Benjamin Ma," the old man said. "You shall call me Mr. Ma or simply Coach." He didn't speak loud, but his voice was commanding. "I shall review the rules. Teams Scarab and White Knight will then mount the course for their first match of the year."

A lump of ice materialized in Eliot's stomach. A match on their first day? He'd expected a warm-up.

"That's not fair," Mitch told Mr. Ma. "No one told us. We're not ready."

Some of the students on Team White Knight snickered.

Mr. Ma looked Mitch over, and then replied, "That is too bad, young man. In life we often find ourselves unprepared. How you perform in such circumstances is the only true test of one's abilities."

Mitch looked like he wanted to protest more, but he only nodded.

"Rule one," Mr. Ma told both groups. "Half of your team members must get to their flag to win. These four must be moving under their own power."

He nodded at the jungle gym. On the very top, two flags unfurled and fluttered, one with a golden scarab, the other with the helmet and lance of White Knight.

They were at least forty feet off the ground.

"Rule two," Mr. Ma said. "You have ten minutes to reach your flag. If neither team gets four members to their flag, then *both* teams record a loss. If both teams get four across, then the team with the lowest time wins."

Eliot knew that winning meant more than just bragging rights. The lowest-ranked teams were cut, and didn't go on to their sophomore year.

"Rule three," Mr. Ma continued. "You may use any means to cross the course. You may use any means to prevent your opponents from doing the same. Magic is allowed, but no weapons, specifically *no* guns, *no* blades, and *no* explosives." His black eyes bored into them. "If I find such contraband, I shall use it *on* the offender."

Eliot was sure he wasn't kidding.

"Questions?" Mr. Ma asked.

"I have a question, sir," Eliot said. He shifted his backpack and unzipped it.

He was the only student who'd brought a pack. He'd had to. At first he'd left Lady Dawn in his locker, but that felt wrong, and when he tried to walk away, his hand burned with pain and the old line of infection reappeared up to his elbow.

Eliot pulled out the battered violin case and opened it for Mr. Ma. "Is *this* a weapon?"

Jeremy and Sarah rolled their eyes.

The people on Team Knight laughed. "Going to play 'Mary Had a Little Lamb'?" one of them asked.

Mr. Ma reached to touch the wood grain, but hesitated.

"Powerful." He assessed Eliot with a look that made him feel like all his secrets were being turned inside out. "But not a weapon, technically, in my class, Mr. Post. She is approved."

The chuckles from the White Knights died.

Eliot took Lady Dawn out. That Queen of Spades playing card was tucked inside the case. He'd put his father's gift there for safekeeping.

He retrieved it and scanned the notes written on it. "The March of the Suicide Queen," Louis had called it.

Eliot hadn't had a chance to play it yet, but the song nonetheless came unbidden to his mind: a fanfare of horns, a swell of strings, and bass kettledrums. It was a military march. He imagined troops gathered upon a field of battle, soldiers with bayoneted rifles and horse-drawn cannon.

He unthinkingly plucked Lady Dawn's strings.

The Ludus Magnus and the rest of the world fell away, and Eliot was alone in the darkness of his imagination, a single spot light illuminating him. A choir of baritone men joined, singing:

Off we go and march to war
sing our song to bloody chore
shoot and stab and rend and kill
Live to march o'er one more hill

Eliot stilled the strings, and the world came back into focus.

The gym structure swayed to the march's rhythm, and then the entire thing leaned toward him as if it wanted him to play more.

Eliot wouldn't, though. That song was too dark. It was about war and killing . . . and while he was certain it could help Team Scarab, it'd be like using artillery at a game of darts.

Everyone stood speechless, staring at him.

The White Knight boy with the shaven head whispered to his teammates, and they nodded—all of them watching Eliot like he was the most dangerous thing they'd ever seen.

Eliot had a bad feeling about that.

Jezebel had held out one hand to Eliot. She retracted the gesture, curling her fingers inward to her chest, and she quickly looked away—but not before Eliot saw her eyes. They were now blue, the color of clear water. Like Julie Marks's had been.

"Team Knight and Team Scarab, ready yourselves," Mr. Ma said. He took out his stopwatch. "Get set. Go!"

19

TEAM SCARAB'S FIRST MATCH

Team Knight and Team Scarab ran for the jungle gym.

Adrenaline pulsed and pounded through Fiona's blood. She raced ahead, and she easily outdistanced them all, except Robert.

He got to the obstacle course first, clambered up a ladder, and turned to make sure she was right behind him.

Fiona grabbed the ladder, but then looked back.

Jeremy and Sarah Covington, Jezebel, Mitch Stephenson, Eliot, and Amanda Lane had scattered across the field. It was total chaos. Eliot had a hard time running with that stupid pack of his.

Team Knight was different. They ran in formation—two four-person teams. One angled left, and one split off to the right side. They had a plan.

"Come on," Robert said. "We need to get up as fast as we can." He scrambled up the ladder.

Sarah and Jeremy ran up to her but ignored the ladder. Instead they tromped along the adjacent spiral that went up a ways and then wormed into the center of the structure.

"Hey!" Fiona said. "Stick together!"

"Middle path, me dearie," Jeremy called back. "Hurry. Knights be taking the high and low paths."

Fiona saw the Knights had done precisely that. One group ran up along a zigzag of stairs—almost as high as Robert now despite his head start. The other group—she just caught a glimpse of them in the lower portion of the course, and then lost them in a tangle of hanging chains.

Jezebel, Mitch, then Eliot, and finally Amanda caught up to her.

"It's a maze," Jezebel said, scrutinizing the structure. "Not all paths lead to our goal, I bet."

"Then which way?" Mitch asked, looking up and squinting.

Amanda was so out of breath, she couldn't speak. She knelt and panted.

Eliot hefted Lady Dawn, and said, "I've got an idea."

Fiona's gut reaction was to tell him to stop playing with that silly violin, that they didn't have time. But with everything she'd seen Eliot do with his music, she figured it was worth the gamble of a few seconds to see what he had in mind.

Jezebel didn't wait, however. She found a knotted rope and pulled herself up hand over hand.

Mitch glanced at her and then to Fiona, indecisive which way to go. He smiled and took a step closer to her. "I'll stay with you guys, if that's okay."

"Great." Mitch hadn't said much to her since school started, but whenever he was around, he had a way of making her feel comfortable. She was glad he was here now.

Eliot ran a thumb over Lady Dawn's strings and then plucked out a whimsical tune.

Fiona smelled popcorn and the burned sugar scent of cotton candy, and then heard on the wind a distant calliope join Eliot's song.

This had something to do with that carnival they'd been in, where they'd fought Perry Millhouse, and where they rescued Amanda.

Amanda went white. Her eyes widened. She backed away from Eliot.

The song was a little musical phrase that repeated and then reflected and inverted and bounced around in Fiona's head. A wonderful invention.

"Where did he learn to play like that?" Mitch asked in awe.

Fiona didn't have an answer for him.

She saw multiples of Eliot prism, as if her eyes were full of tears. She saw the obstacle course blur with a hundred different twisting paths. It was like the mirror maze in the carnival; that's what Eliot's music was about.

The jungle gym creaked and pinged. The scuffed aluminum ladder shone like it was new—and then a dozen rungs up, there was a set of monkey bars whose tarnished brass cleared and gleamed as if just polished—and where those ended, a balance beam of scuffed and scratched wood smoothed into gleaming mahogany as she watched.

He was finding the path through the course.

"The quickest way to the flag," Eliot said as he played. "Go. Quick. I'll keep playing."

Mitch started up the ladder, and then waited for Fiona and Amanda.

Fiona wasn't sure. It was a great idea, but she didn't like leaving Eliot by himself.

How else were they going to win, though?

She and Eliot locked eyes. It'd be okay; they both knew how to take care of themselves if they had to.

"I can't do this," Amanda whispered. She looked miserable, sick from the brief sprint, terrified at the height of the imposing course, one hand clutching the side of her head, trying to block out Eliot's music. "Let me stay. I'd just slow you down."

"Keep your eyes open at least," Fiona told her . . . a little more nastily than she had intended.

Fiona and Mitch then mounted the ladder, climbed up—and then swung onto the monkey bars, following Eliot's gleaming path.

Mitch got onto the balance beam, braced one hand on a railing, and extended his other hand to Fiona.

She took it and felt perfectly safe with him here—she looked down—even though "here" was a precarious twenty feet high.

They stepped across the beam, followed its arc shape up and then down in a half-moon trajectory and landed on a platform held by a steel pole. The thing swayed but held their weight.

Eliot looked small on the ground, his music tinny and far away . . . but it still worked: Among the tangles of woven rope netting that went up from the platform, one section looked new, its knots squared and firm and sturdy.

"Your brother's a miracle worker," Mitch said, and started up.

"He's something, that's for sure," she replied.

If they'd been smart, they would have had Eliot find the path ahead of time, and they could all have gone up together.

Fiona scanned the course and spotted Jezebel ten feet higher, where her rope ended in a solid concrete ceiling. She was stuck.

Robert was very high now . . . almost to their flag. Good for him.

Should she have gone with him in the first place? That would have given them two at their goal. Nearly half a win. She didn't see Jeremy or Sarah.

Half of Team White Knight, though, were almost to their flag. They worked together, helping each other along, and they were all looking for the best path . . . keeping an eye out for an attack from Team Scarab as well? It was a smart strategy.

Fiona clambered over the top of the cargo netting and into a tube made of chain link. It was rickety, sloped down and then up and then sideways, spilling out into a series of hand-powered lifts: a bucket and rope and pulleys that would carry them almost to Robert's position.

In a minute, they could be all caught up.

A breeze rocked the gym. Fiona clutched onto the chain and felt her stomach in her throat.

She looked down, for a moment not being able to see Eliot . . . then she found him. Tiny and playing and still there.

But she saw something else that made her heart skip a beat: the missing half of Team White Knight. They were on the ground and moving toward her bother.

In a flash, she understood. Their strategy was to send one half up—fast sprinters—and let one half lag behind to slow down the opposition. And right now, the most vulnerable target was her trouble-magnet of a brother.

They were going to clobber him.

"Eliot!" she yelled.

Her voice was lost in the breeze. Eliot kept his head down, playing.

"I see them, too," Mitch said, his normally reassuring tone heavy with concern. "There's no way to get to him in time."

The Knights moved carefully . . . probably because they knew magic when they heard it and didn't want to give Eliot a chance to turn on them.

Amanda just sat there, listening. Utterly useless.

Fiona's anger came. It spilled through her blood, molten and pulsing and erupting along every nerve.

She turned to Mitch. "Get to the flag. You can't follow the way I'm going."

Fiona stretched the rubber band on her wrist and sliced through the wire cage.

Without a moment's hesitation, she jumped—free fall for a heartbeat—then impacted on the platform below.

The wood splintered and cracked. Pain exploded along her shins, and her shirt ripped.

These distractions were quickly blotted out by her swelling anger.

Her father's words echoed in her mind once more: *"Within you burns the fury of all the Hells, unquenchable and unstoppable."*

She flipped around to the underside of the platform, grabbed the supporting pole, and slid thirty feet down. She landed so hard, her sneakers made craters.

She stalked onto the field.

"Hey!" Fiona shouted at two closest Knights, a boy and a girl.

They turned, shock on their faces; then the boy regained his wits and spoke to the girl. It was Tamara from the locker room. She smiled and moved to Fiona while the boy continued toward Eliot.

Amanda heard Fiona's shout, however. She glanced about wildly, now seeing the danger: three White Knight boys had her and Eliot surrounded. She screamed.

That scream broke Eliot out of his trance. He looked up, turned all around, taking in the three boys closing in. He hesitated; his fingers twitched.

Meanwhile, Tamara blocked Fiona's path and set one hand on the ground. The grass where she touched turned gray and crumpled to dust—a circle of death that spread outward.

Around Fiona, however, the yellowed grass greened, wiggled, bursting forth with life, and growing in thick tangles about her feet.

She took one step, but the grass snaked and laced about her, holding fast.

Tamara laughed.

Fiona knelt to cut the offending runners, but as soon as she did, shoots gripped her thigh, pulled the one hand she'd set onto the ground, holding it.

She tugged. The grass ripped out . . . but immediately grew new, stronger roots.

Tendrils wormed along her wrist and up to her elbow. She yanked as hard as she could, but she felt the anger slipping from her . . . becoming panic, hot in her throat.

Fiona glanced up. The three boys were almost on Eliot.

Eliot flicked his fingers over his violin, and a dissonant chord distorted the air between him and the closest boy—throwing the boy backward as if he'd been swatted with a giant invisible hand.

But that's all the chance the other two needed to rush in.

One tackled Eliot; the other kicked Lady Dawn from his grasp.

Tamara walked near Fiona. As she did so, the grass pulled harder, pulled her closer to the ground, and twined about her neck. Tamara was going to make her eat dirt . . . or strangle her.[21]

"Remember, little dung scarab," Tamara said, "in gym class, we can use *any* means to stop our opponents— even if that means *killing* them. Bet you wish you had that Infernal with you now."

She was bluffing. Had to be.

Try as she might, though, Fiona couldn't summon her hate again; it was like trying to make herself hiccup.

She strained against the pulling grass . . . helpless.

Fiona heard a girl's voice: "The Infernal *is* here, fool."

She turned her head. Jezebel was five paces away. Her expression was cool and implacable—save her eyes, which boiled with caustic venom. The grass around her, instead of grabbing, bent toward her and bowed in supplication.

Jezebel crossed the distance to Tamara in two quick strides and backhanded her, sending the girl end over end through the air.

---

21. Tamara Pritchard, part of the Dreaming Families, and infamous for her use of Life/Death dual magics, was born with gifts we could scarcely imagine. Had her focus been magical rather than social engineering during those early years . . . she would have been a real threat to us. *The Secret Red Diaries of Sarah Covington, Third Edition,* Sarah Covington, Mariposa Printers, Dublin.

Tamara landed in the sod and didn't move.

"Help," Fiona whispered.

Jezebel looked down with contempt. "Help yourself. You have all you need at your fingertips." She moved toward Eliot. "Do what you do best and *cut*."

Cut? There was nothing at her fingertips besides grass.

. . . Which were very much like threads. Heck, they were even called *blades* of grass. She'd been such an idiot.

Fiona focused, felt the edges of every grass shoot touching her, saw their delicate edges—and pressed until they sharpened and focused to a laser-thin line—

—that cut—each other—the ground—everything, slicing itself into a million wriggling shreds of confetti.

Fiona got up and ran to Eliot.

One of the boys sat with his full weight on her brother's shoulders, pinning him facefirst in the grass. The other boy strode to Lady Dawn. And the third boy moved toward Amanda . . . who, to her credit, was at least *trying* to outmaneuver the bully around a pole and get to Eliot.

The boy on Eliot reared back to hit Eliot's head.

Jezebel got to him first—tackled the boy—a blur of motion—they rolled together once on the ground. There was the snap of breaking bone.

The Infernal got up. The boy didn't move.

Eliot shakily got to his feet.

Fiona joined him. "You okay?"

"I think so," Eliot grunted, rubbing the back of his neck. "If my head's still on straight." He gazed riveted on his violin. "Hey! Don't touch her!"

The other boy picked up Lady Dawn.

A string snapped and sliced the boy's arm—cutting the vein at his wrist.

"Holy—!" The boy dropped her and clutched his wrist, blood dribbling out.

A whistle trilled, and that sent shivers down Fiona's spine.

Mr. Ma had appeared on the field (although Fiona had not seen him anywhere close). "That is the match," he declared. "Halt all activities."

Mr. Ma pulled out a handheld radio and called for medics. He went to the bleeding White Knight student and sprinkled a powder on his wrist, which staunched the flow of blood.

"Thank goodness it's over," Fiona breathed.

She turned to thank Jezebel, but the Infernal was already walking off the field.

"Did we win?" Eliot asked.

Mr. Ma now had an extinguisher in hand. He blasted a jet of frozen carbon dioxide at a fire licking a wooden pole on the obstacle course.

Had one of the White Knights tried to burn something? Fiona hadn't seen any of them set it, but who else? What wouldn't these people do to win?

The other four White Knight boys and girls slid down ropes in formation.

Robert, Mitch, Jeremy, and Sarah clambered down along different routes . . . and from the long looks on their faces, Mr. Ma didn't have to say who'd won.

How could this have gone so wrong?

"What happened?" she asked Mitch.

"Didn't get there in time," he said with a shrug, but otherwise seemed unfazed. "Once the music stopped, it took me longer than I thought to find the right way."

Sarah stalked up to her. "Next time you be halfway to the flag, I suggest—strongly suggest—you keep going. The match would have been over in a blink if you'd let them have your brother a wee bit." She trounced off.

Fiona was too shocked to reply.

She couldn't image what those four White Knights would have done to Eliot. They would have put him in the hospital for sure.

Maybe that was the point.

A few broken arms, and you could reduce the number of opponents on the other team—maybe permanently, so if you had to play that team again, there'd be fewer of them, and a better chance to win.

Logical. And horrifying.

Robert, covered in sweat, came up to her and Eliot. "You guys all right?"

"We're fine," she told him.

Why hadn't Robert stayed with them? Had he wanted to win so badly that he'd forgotten everything else?

Looking at him as he stood panting, soaked, a faint bruise under one eye, she wondered again just what he was doing at Paxington. He wasn't interested in books and learning. Robert lived to ride.

Before she could figure out how to even ask Robert about any of this, Mr. Ma spoke.

"Three at Scarab's flag," he announced. "Four for White Knight at seven minutes thirteen seconds. A moderately good time. Win for the Knights." Mr. Ma nodded at their team, and then looked over to Fiona and Eliot. "A loss for Scarab."

The White Knight boys and girls exchanged high fives and went to their injured teammates to help the medics dress wounds and get them off the field. None of them spared Fiona another look.

And why should they? They'd lost.

"Too many weak links on this team," Jeremy said bitterly, and walked off the field.

Eliot looked like he'd been struck.

Fiona didn't like the way Jeremy had said that . . . it sounded like a threat, and she wondered if the students on the other teams were the *only* ones she'd have to worry about.

20

❧

LITTLE WHITE LIE

Eliot was sure Jeremy and Sarah Covington blamed him . . . with their averted glances and cold shoulders all week. And yet, they still spoke to Fiona, and Jeremy always tried to open doors for her.

As far as they were concerned, he was just her "little brother," the kid with the violin who had caused half their team to lag behind and lose their first match.

He sat in the back of Miss Westin's Mythology 101 class. This week she continued her lecture of the mortal magical families. He'd learned about the Kaleb clan and the Scalagari family.[22]

---

22. The Scalagari family is renowned for its weavers and fine tailors. They employ highly guarded methods to weave magical aspects into cloth. Their camel hair overcoats, for example, are impervious to bullet or blade, and are said to have the "strength and weight" of an entire mountain woven into their feather-soft fabric. The Scalagaris also have a darker side, reputably connected to the criminal underworld. From ancestral estates on Sicily and the isle of Nero Basilica, it is said they operate gambling, extortion, and smuggling rings (under constant investigation by Interpol; no charges, however, have ever been bought to court). *Gods of the First and Twenty-first Century,*

Everyone at Paxington was special in their own way. Some families had political clout, others had powerful magic, and some had a pedigree that stretched back to antiquity.

And while Eliot, at least in theory, had *all* these things, no one could know (thanks to the League's stupid rules).

Even if there weren't rules, Eliot wasn't sure it would matter. If people knew who and what he was—*especially* if people knew who and what he was—that would just make it worse. He'd be the Immortal hero kid with all the power, family, and political connections who *still* lost the match for Team Scarab.

Miss Westin ended the lecture and wrote an extra-credit reading assignment on John Dee on the blackboard.

Fiona sat next to Eliot. While she was completely absorbed, scribbling this down, he grabbed his notes and slunk out of class.

"Wait a second," Fiona hissed after him.

Eliot kept going. He wanted to be alone.

Slipping through the blackout curtains and double doors of the auditorium, he blinked in the too-bright sunlight after being in the shadows for the last two hours.

Or maybe losing the match *wasn't* his fault.

What if everyone on his team shared the blame? What if losing was as much Jeremy and Sarah's fault for not meeting ahead of time and coming up with a plan? They were the ones who were supposed to know everything.

Eliot had actually helped Fiona and Mitch find the right path before getting ambushed.

What if Team Knight had just been better prepared?

As his eyes adjusted to the noontime sun, he saw that he wasn't the only one to have left early.

Jezebel was here as well.

Last week, when she had looked at him as he held Lady Dawn—at that particular moment—Jezebel had looked *exactly* like Julie . . . down to her blue eyes.

The fantasy of Jezebel being Julie vanished as Jezebel tilted her head, blinking in the sunlight, getting her bearings. Her features were too sharp, cheekbones pushed up higher . . . and, of course, she was an Infernal protégée.

Julie had just been . . . well, Julie. Normal. Mortal. Nice.

Concern creased Jezebel's otherwise smooth forehead as if she was worried she would be seen. Then she spotted him. Her eyes narrowed with disgust. She turned and walked off in the opposite direction.

But that look—it was the same annoyed, you're-under-my-skin-look that Julie had given him . . . just before she had kissed him the first time.

Eliot was totally confused now.

He followed her. "Jezebel!" he called out.

Her stride faltered, only a single step, but it was enough to know she'd heard him.

She continued walking, increasing her pace.

Eliot trotted behind her. "Thanks for the other day. You know . . . gym class. You saved my neck."

"Begone, wormfood." Her voice was full of icy indifference. "I've nothing to say to you."

He'd expected this. He'd be defensive, too, if everyone treated him the way the other students had treated her—all the whispering, the leering, and the innuendo—just because of her family.

Eliot had, however, seen Hell for himself. Maybe there was a good reason to treat her differently.

But wasn't he like her, too? At least part Infernal?

Maybe it was time to trust someone . . . introduce himself. There were no stupid League rules that prevented him from telling anyone about his *Infernal* side. He and Jezebel might even be distant cousins, for all he knew.

"I'm Eliot Post," he said, this time quietly. "I'm half Infernal. On my father's side."

Jezebel slowed. She still didn't look his way, but she pursed her lips as if deciding something.

"Lucifer's son," he said.

They entered the corridor that led to the quartz-paved quad. Columns of veined marble cast crisscrossing shadows along their path.

"You are a fool, Eliot Post." She quickened her stride.

Eliot's strength left him. How much rejection was a guy supposed to take before he finally got the hint?

"Okay, no problem," he said. Then so softly that even he barely heard: "You just reminded me of someone I cared about. A lot. Someone I miss."

Jezebel halted half in and half out of the shadows.

She trembled. One hand made a fist. One hand reached out, fingers splayed.

Eliot felt a tug in his center: a connection.

Something inside him was drawn to something within her. . . .

"Julie?" He took a tentative step toward her. "It *is* you, somehow, isn't it?"

A shuddering breath escaped her, and she turned to him. Her fist clenched tighter, knuckles popping. But her open hand reached for him. Her face quivered with rage *and* longing; one eye was green—the other blue, and from it, a single tear marked her cheek.

"Maybe," she said.

The effort of that one word seemed to quench her anger. "Once I might have been Julie, but you don't know what I've done since then—or plan to do," she said, her words intensifying. "Or what I really am now."

Eliot met her hand with his, and took it. Her flesh was warm and soft and yielding.

Her face was a mix of Infernal and mortal, Jezebel and the Julie Marks he knew.

He wanted to tell her how much he had missed her. How wonderful that she was here now with him.

The thing in his center, pulling him closer to her, however, cooled and curled inward—repulsed.

"You lied to me." He dropped her hand. "I mean, you are Infernal. There's no way you could have lied about *that* in front of Miss Westin and got away with it. So that means in Del Sombra you weren't really Julie Marks?"

Her blue eye dissolved into translucent green once more. The tear upon her human flesh evaporated.

"There is *no* Julie Marks," she told him, her voice hoarse.

"You pretended to be the manager at Ringo's," he said, "and said we'd run away together to Hollywood." Eliot's tone hardened. "Was *everything* a lie, then? Did you even ever like me?"

Jezebel's open hand closed, and trembled, as if barely restraining it from violence. Her gaze dropped to the floor.

"Tell me the truth," Eliot demanded.

The shadows in the corridor deepened and angled— became bands of absolute dark slashed by golden sunlight. Eliot stood half in and half out of the shade.

Jezebel, however, was now fully immersed in the darkness.

"You want the truth?" she whispered sweetly, but there was cruelty in her voice as well.

Eliot had a feeling this was much more than a simple question. It was something Infernal. A ritual he didn't understand, like signing a contract in blood. It was dangerous.

He couldn't stop himself, though. He had to know.

"I do," he said.

She glared at him for a heartbeat. Her hands dropped to her side. The air chilled. "How can you be so smart and so stupid at the same time?"

Eliot had often wondered this very thing, but wasn't about to admit it.

"I was Julie Marks long ago," she told him. "I lived in Atlanta, ran away, made many foolish choices, and died of a heroin overdose. I wasted my life."

To hear her speak of her death so casually horrified Eliot.

A boy and girl from their Mythology 101 class passed by, shot curious glances their way, and hurried along.

"I died," she continued, "and I went to Hell, the Poppy Lands of Queen Sealiah. I won't bore you with the torment heaped upon my unworthy mortal soul there, but just know that I was picked by my Queen and given a chance to live again."

The chill from the shadows made Eliot shiver.

This *was* the truth, though—he sensed that much— and it tasted addictively sweet to him.

More students passed them, and gave Jezebel a wide berth, wanting to avoid those preternaturally cold shadows.

"That is when I came to you, Eliot, darling." She

inched closer, the shadows dragged along with her, and her voice rose over the murmurs in the corridor. "I was sent to seduce you, to trick you to come back to the lightless realms. I was bait, which you so eagerly tasted."

Eliot took a step back.

"But you left . . . without me."

She paused; confusion crossed her features, then it cleared. "Yes, another in a long string of mistakes I've made. Instead of seducing, I was seduced by your music . . . into believing there was something more, something better."

"It's not too late," Eliot told her. "There's still hope. There's always hope."

"Like there was hope when I ran away to protect you? When they caught me and dragged me back to Hell? Like there was hope when they did so many unpleasant, unspeakable things to me to repay my hope-filled *kindness*?"

Jezebel laughed. It was the sound of breaking glass and ancient glacier ice crackling. It was a thousand prancing, dancing booted feet that crushed dreams.

"There is no hope in Hell, Eliot Post. And there is no longer hope in my heart. I am a creature of the Lower Realms, reborn into the Clan Sealiah. The venomous blood of the Queen of Poppies forever flows through my veins. Dare not tempt me with your vile hope ever again, if you desire to draw another breath."

Every student in the hall had stopped to listen to this.

Eliot retreated another step and backed into a column.

Jezebel leaned closer. "You are a complete, utter moron. A fool of such sterling caliber, you could be the Prince of Incompetence. I wish I'd never met you."